MEAT

Michael Bray

Copyright © Michael Bray 2014

The author or authors assert their moral right under the Copyright, Designs and Patents Act, 1988, to be identified as the author or authors of this work.

All Rights reserved. No part of this publication may be reproduced, copied, stored in a retrieval system, or transmitted, in any form or by any means, without the prior written consent of the author or publisher, nor be otherwise circulated in any form of binding or cover other than that in which it is published and without a similar condition being imposed on the subsequent purchaser.

CONTENTS

Delivery *
Stakeout*
The Foot **
Curiosity & The Cat *
Bernard **
Sally & Ellie *
Making Plans **
Silas*
Bo
Failed Escape **
Confrontation **
No More Favours **
Pact*
Nicu **
The Impossible Ultimatum
Lee/Accusations **
Leena
Sally's Promise*
What Happened With Nicu **
Mark **
Negotiations
Chaos **
Endgame
Author Notes

* Newly added chapter
** Indicates extended content.

*"But if you're gonna dine with them cannibals,
Sooner or later, darling, you're gonna get eaten."*
— *Nick Cave*

DELIVERY

Luke Jones had been homeless for seven years. Neglect as a child had caused him to rebel, which in turn had led to him being kicked out of home by his abusive drunk of a father on his seventeenth birthday. Too old for foster care, and considered damaged goods by those who were supposed to be friends and family, he had drifted from place to place. First begging friends to let him sleep on their floors or sofas, then as each welcome was worn out, took to sleeping rough. Soon enough, the favours dried up, and sleeping on the streets had become the norm. Part of his routine.

He had watched the new supermarket take shape over the last couple of weeks and still, couldn't understand why any company with any sense would open a store in such a shitty area. The other businesses around it were either closed or barely keeping their heads above water, struggling to make ends meet ever since the new megamall opened its doors and catered for everything a person might need, all under one roof. For whatever reason, whoever owned this new place seemed to have bucked the trend and the bright lights of the mall in favour of a shitty, run down part of town like this. Luke stood across the street, hands in pockets, hood pulled up over his face. Grueber's World of Food, proclaimed the illuminated sign above the automatic doors. As confused as he was about why anyone would open a place in the area, he didn't really care. His stomach growled at him and reminded him why he had come here. Supermarkets meant food. And food was something he was desperate for. He approached the store casually, giving it a cursory glance as he walked straight past the entrance. He had learned the hard way that shoplifting was only asking for trouble, especially when he knew he looked like shit. He knew all too well that the staff would give him the thousand yard stare as soon as he walked through the door, especially at night when security guards tended to be on the lookout for people like him. Instead of entering the store, he walked to the alleyway next to it, keeping close to the wall as he walked into the shadow draped depths. It was a cool night, and the breeze was doing a fine job of pushing the unique stench of food waste around with sickening efficiency. He caught a whiff of rotten meat and wrinkled his nose. It was nothing new to him, of course. He had long since grown used to living with the extreme smells that came with living rough. Some of the places where he had stayed were barely fit for animals, let alone people. Thinking about it for too long could only lead to doubt, which in the end made the difference between death or survival. And he *was* a survivor. A stubborn one at that. He did what he had to in order to live, in order to keep seeing the sun rise. He wasn't proud of some of the lengths he had gone to in the past, but in his situation, there was no room for pride anyway. All that mattered, was getting something to eat. He could see the supermarket's loading door, a corrugated steel shutter which rattled when the wind touched it. He passed it, barely giving it a glance. His interest was in the dumpster beside it. Luke walked to it and opened the lid, holding his breath against the smell and hoping to find something good. He knew supermarkets tended to throw away their foods once they reached their best before dates, but he also knew well enough the food was good for up to another two weeks after that date. Whilst his fellow homeless folk scrambled around the soup kitchen, Luke had a ready-made supply of unopened, good-to-eat food from most of the supermarkets across town. He still had to be cautious, though, as getting caught would be an end to his little adventure. Even though the food had been thrown away, most of the supermarkets had taken an aversion to people going through their rubbish in search of food, and many had installed padlocks to keep people like Luke away. He pushed his way through the black plastic bags, pulling a few open in search of the good stuff when his world became illuminated with the unmistakable glare of headlights.

Reacting on instinct, he slammed the dumpster lid and hid against the wall, watching as the crimson truck reversed down the alleyway. It was emblazoned with the Grueber's logo in white on its side and came to a halt level with the raised loading area. Luke watched as the steel shutter he had walked past just a few moments ago clicked to life with an electronic whine and began to roll open. A stocky man walked onto the loading area. Luke watched as the delivery driver climbed out of the cab, strode up the ramp and handed over a clipboard. The man from the store looked over it and signed it before handing it back to the driver.

Delivery time.

Luke thought this might be a good chance to snag some fresh goods, maybe even some booze. All he would have to do is wait until the worker was loading stock in and the van was unguarded, and he would be able to make his move. Adrenaline surged through him, and he couldn't help but grin at the thought of what he was about to do. He watched as the delivery driver unlocked the truck, and swung open the back doors. When he saw what was inside, Luke forgot all about stealing food, being cold and tired and even about his hunger. All he could do was stare.

It was filled with people.

They were naked and bound together by the feet and hands. Luke watched in horror as the frightened cargo shuffled off the truck and into the loading bay. He counted twenty in all, aged between twenty and fifty as best he could guess. The stocky man ushered them through the loading bay doors, counting them off as they passed. Some were crying, others impassive and silent as they did as they were instructed. They were all shepherded into the store, and the stocky man and the delivery driver exchanged small talk. Luke stared and wondered what to do. He hated dealing with the police, but he knew this wasn't an ordinary situation, and he would have to tell somebody what was going on here. He shifted position, trying to get a look into the store, but the instant he moved, both the stocky man and the delivery driver stopped talking, and looked right in his direction.

He froze, and held his breath as he ducked out of sight behind the dumpster. He realised then it was a dead end. There was no way out other than the way he had come. He strained his ears but could hear nothing but the drone of distant traffic. He waited. Time seemed to stretch out to infinity, and when he built up the courage to peek around the edge of the dumpster, he wasn't sure if he was relieved or even more afraid.

Both the stocky man and the delivery driver were gone. The loading bay was still open, and the engine of the truck was still running, but the alleyway was empty. Luke cast his eyes over the shadowy recess of the alley, places where a person might be able to hide if they were so inclined. The years spent living on the streets had sharpened his instincts, and they screamed at him now to run. He greedily eyed the street thirty feet away. He could make it. He knew it. As was his way, he didn't pause to think and lurched off into a run. He darted towards the delivery truck, knowing he would feel safer when he was past it and out into the open air. He focused on the street at the end of the alleyway and ran, focusing on nothing else but his freedom.

It happened as he passed the open loading bay door. He saw a flicker of movement, a shadow against the light spilling out into the alleyway, but by then it was too late. The short life of Luke Jones was over before he felt his throat being torn open, and before his body was catapulted into the side of the truck, his arms and legs flailing like a rag doll as he crumbled to the ground. His dead eyes stared at the floor as the stocky man strode over, and with little effort or care, picked up the body, hoisted it over his shoulder and walked towards the loading bay door. He tossed the corpse over the threshold, paused to look up and down the alleyway, and then activated the controls to close the shutter, plunging the alleyway back into shadow draped silence.

STAKEOUT

The pale green sedan was parked across the street from the store. Its two occupants watched as people entered sporadically. The driver, a wiry African American, licked his lips and scratched at his beard as he peered at the store.

"I don't know, man. I don't think I like this."

The man beside him was taller, and unlike his nervous partner seemed both less afraid and more determined. He pulled his long hair into a ponytail and secured it, then checked his watch.

"It'll be fine, pal," he said, his accent thick Irish. "It's now or never."

"You sure about this? If we do this you know there's no going back."

"You know as well as I do this is the only choice we have."

"Whatever you say. Just be careful."

"Will do. No need to panic yet. I wanna go in there and take a look around first. If I don't like it, we can call it off. You just wait here till I come back."

"You got it, buddy," the driver said as the long-haired man got out of the car and crossed the road, pausing to let a blue Passat pull into one of the spaces out front of the store. He took one last look over his shoulder then went inside.

II

The man in the blue Passat got out of the car and was about to head into the store when his cell phone rang. He fished it out of his jeans and looked at the display. His wife's name flashed in blue as the phone vibrated in its demand to be answered. But he didn't want to get into another argument, not when the one they had just finished had been so volatile. He loved her, of that, there was no doubt, but such was their similarity to each other when they argued, their respective stubbornness made them both fight to get the last word. He leaned on his car, and couldn't believe the almighty argument had started because he had used up the last of the milk without replacing it. Of course, he had to allow for the pregnancy, and the fact her hormones were all askew, but he didn't like to lose, and had argued his case, which quickly descended into a bout of throwing personal insults at each other. He had stormed out of the house, telling her he might be better off with someone who wasn't such a bitch. Now he had calmed, he, of course, regretted it, but at the time, felt an exhilarating sense of victory when he saw the pained look in her eyes when he closed the door on his way out. He was sure he had gone too far, and even though he wanted to take the call and apologise, he wasn't sure it was sufficiently diffused enough for that to happen. He looked at the handset, the vibrating 'Stacey' on screen demanding his attention. He hovered briefly over the answer key, and then changed his mind and rejected the call. He still needed to cool off himself a little bit yet and thought it would be better they talk in person, once he had replaced the milk. He also really wanted a nice steak or something for dinner. He stuffed the phone into his pocket, then walked towards the store.

III

On the opposite side of the street, the wiry African American realised what it was that had been bothering him since they had arrived. Although they had been watching the place for almost an hour and had seen a lot of people go into the store, not a single one had come out again. Something about that made his stomach vault, and he eyed the place nervously as if seeing it through fresh eyes. The building made him incredibly uncomfortable, and yet he could see no reason for it. He had been telling himself it was just a building, a supermarket just like any other, but with each rationalisation, he asked himself another question. Why were there no windows? Why had nobody come out? Why had nobody known this place was being built here? More to the point, why build it here in the middle of nowhere, unless there was a reason to be anonymous?

Whatever it was, he was glad he was on the outside and hoped his friend would get the hell out of there soon so they could be on their way. Across the street, someone else walked into Grueber's, and still, nobody came out.

The Foot

It was a foot. A human foot. Garrett wasn't sure quite how to react and looked up and down the length of the supermarket walkway before turning his attention back to the appendage in the freezer. At first, he thought it was a prank – perhaps the next great TV show idea designed to fool the unwitting public- and yet he knew it wasn't. The foot in the freezer didn't look like a prop. It wasn't made of rubber. There were too many details. Ghostly veins were visible just under the skin, and the underside of the toes was cracked and well worn. The full magnitude of the situation hit home, and as if to prove to himself it wasn't a case of his imagination getting out of hand, he deliberately looked away, focusing his attention on his shoes, allowing his mind to empty and see clearly. He knew how perception could easily fool the brain into seeing things which weren't real, and he was sure this was exactly that. He turned his gaze back to the freezer, his stomach plummeting to his shoes as he saw how his initial reaction seemed to have been- as impossible as it seemed – correct. The foot was nestled between the vast array of chickens and chunky cuts of beef and housed in a plastic tray on a bed of lettuce. The entire shrink-wrapped appendage had been cut off below the ankle, and the fleshy underside seasoned with pepper. The sandwich he had eaten for lunch quivered a little in his stomach when he realised the foot—as unfathomable as it seemed—was quite real. He leaned closer to examine the label on the front of the package.

Grueber's Free Range human foot!
White male left foot,
Pre-washed and ready to cook.
Delicious, hot or cold!

Garrett saw with dismay that the freezer was filled with severed feet of all races, all sizes, and priced according to weight. It wasn't just feet. The more he actually looked, the more he saw. Hands sold individually or in pairs. Racks of human ribs which still had the skin on one side for 'easy roast crackling'. He felt a dizzy giggle dance up to his throat and had to force himself to swallow it back down.

All thoughts of replenishing the milk were gone, and he discreetly looked around trying to put some kind of rational context to the situation which might enable his mind to cope. He expected to see more horrors, things which would look more at home in the kitchen of Jeffrey

Dahmer rather than plain old Ray Garrett, and yet the rest of the supermarket looked perfectly normal and as unremarkable as expected. It followed the same tried and tested design model as countless other markets all over the world with its polished floors and wide, well-stocked shelves that had all the temptations discreetly placed at eye level. It was all so... *ordinary*. In numb disbelief, he glanced up and down the length of the aisle to see if anybody else but him had noticed what was happening. There was an old couple at the furthest end of the store, the man pushing the trolley whilst the woman carefully checked off the goods on their list. Garrett couldn't see anything unusual in the inventory they had gathered so far, and certainly no body parts. Either way, they didn't appear to be at all concerned that the new local supermarket seemed to be trading in human flesh. He desperately wanted to move, to do anything not to draw attention to his horror, but his own feet—perhaps in protest at the treatment of its fellow appendages— refused to co-operate. He glanced at his reflection in the glass-fronted freezer doors and saw a pale faced, open-mouthed parody of himself looking back.

"Hey, man, take it easy."

The voice in his ear almost made him scream outright, and did nothing for his already fraying nerves. Garrett spun on his heel and was face to face with the man who almost scared him half to death.

He was one of those indie rocker types with sandy hair down to his collar and over his ears that was styled to look messy but somehow came across as incredibly stylish. He was effortlessly pulling off the '*too-cool-to-care*' look. His girlfriend—a thin and naturally attractive blonde with nervous eyes— hung on his arm and kept her head low. Garrett tried to look the indie rocker in the eye but was met with his own funhouse mirror reflection in his aviator glasses.

"What do you mean?" Garrett muttered, still trying to gather his thoughts together and rationalise the situation as aviator leaned closer.

"I said, take it easy, or you'll give us all up." Aviator tried to smile, but it came off as a nervous twitch of the cheek.

"What are you talking about?"

Aviator fidgeted from one foot to the other, and Garrett realised the kid was scared. He nodded to towards the freezer. No words were necessary.

"It's a joke, surely, right?" Garrett whispered.

"I wish it was, man. I truly do."

"I don't understand. I…" Garrett began and then couldn't think of anything else to say. Instead, he looked at the kid in the aviator glasses, who now wore a nervous grin and was absently scratching at his cheek, leaving an angry red mark as he stared at the freezer full of human meat.

"You see it, though, don't you?" Aviator asked. "I mean, you know what those are, right?"

Garrett didn't know what to do. It all felt too unreal to say out loud, and he couldn't help himself from sneaking another quick glance of his own at the shrink-wrapped limbs in the freezer. He settled for a nod.

"Pretty crazy, huh?" Aviator said. "We actually didn't see the feet. It was the pickled fingers in aisle three that first got us to pay attention."

He jammed a thumb over his shoulder as he said it and offered Garrett another attempt at a grin that looked as if it were supposed to be confident but came out instead as a frightened grimace.

"What the hell's happening in here?" Garrett whispered.

"I don't know, man. We just called in here on our way to the movies. You ever shopped here before?"

Garrett shook his head. "No. I didn't even know this place was here. Last time I came by this way, this was an empty plot."

Aviator took off his glasses, and Garrett saw under the wannabe rock star illusion that he was just a frightened boy. His blue eyes darted from Garrett to the fridges, then the aisle—which apart from them was empty.

"Hey, what's your name?" Garrett asked.

"Mark. And this is Leena," he said, motioning to his girlfriend who, apart from the odd furtive glance, was still staring at the floor.

"I'm Ray, Ray Garrett."

Mark nodded, and the two stood in silence for a few awkward seconds.

"Walk with me," Mark said quietly.

"Why?"

"Because they are watching us." Garrett started to turn his head, but Mark saw it and stopped him.

"No, don't look. Just walk. Come on, this way."

With no reason to argue and not yet able to quite deal with the situation, Garrett did as he was told and followed the couple as they headed away from the gruesome contents of the freezers.

They walked past the regular meats: the pork joints, rib eyes, and the legs of lamb. Every now and then, they would pass something not so ordinary.

A large blister pack of human liver.

A display of jars containing milky, pickled eyeballs.

A shelf full of plastic containers containing a nasty, fatty liquid labelled simply 'human dripping'.

"We have to get out of here," Garrett said, his voice sounding like it was an octave or so too high even to him. Mark shook his head.

"It's not that easy. Someone tried it earlier. An old guy. He came in and saw the feet. He was standing pretty much where you were when you first saw them, but he freaked and ran back towards the entrance. They cornered him off, and two of the staff members ushered him into a room in the back. We watched for a while, but he never came back. I… I don't think they will ever let us out of here."

"They?"

"The staff."

Garrett felt his stomach do yet another dizzy rotation as Mark's words sunk in. He also realised with dismay that the store – much like any other – had only one exit and no windows.

"How long have you been in here?" he asked, pushing such worrying thoughts aside.

"A while now. We're trying to put a show on of actually shopping for groceries, but I don't think we are fooling anyone. It's all a big fucking act and they know it."

"Surely someone has gone for help, called the police or…" His wife's face projected itself into Garrett's mind, and he started to scramble for his phone. "I need to call my wife. We need to call the police…"

"You don't get it, do you?" Mark said, looking at Garrett with that expression which was part grin, part grimace.

"What?"

"You can't call anyone. Nobody can help us now. They're letting people in, but so far nobody has been allowed to leave."

"But if I can just call home…"

"Phones don't work in here. We already tried."

Garrett looked at his handset, hoping against hope Mark was wrong. Yet, the display read simply 'No signal'. He shoved the phone back into his pocket.

"What do we do, man? How do we get out of here?" Mark asked.

He watched Garrett, waiting for his reply, searching for hope or reassurance. Garrett had none of either to give and so avoided both question and eye contact as they walked.

"They can't just keep us here," he said eventually. "It's a damn supermarket, not a prison."

It wasn't what Mark wanted to hear, or exactly the kind of statement Garrett had hoped to give. Even so, it was the best he could do under the circumstances.

"I'm not so sure you're right."

"What are you saying?"

"I think this place, this building, is like one of those plants. You know, those exotic ones that entice insects to crawl inside by secreting a sweet smell, and then they close up behind them? Well, I think that's what this place is. It's here to draw us in."

"I don't understand," Garrett said.

"Well, it would be easy. This place is a big box with only one way in or out. Everyone shops, man, everyone. It doesn't matter if you are the richest of the rich, or poorest of the poor. All they had to do was set up shop and wait."

"And that makes us the insects," Garrett whispered, nauseated by the unreality of it all.

"Exactly. Which makes me think we're all in the shit here."

"You don't know that. We might be okay," Garrett said without conviction.

"I'd love to believe that, but look at it this way. These guys have to get their meat from somewhere."

Garrett could find no suitable response to that and said nothing. They had moved away from the meat and into the next aisle, which was stacked with canned goods. Although he didn't want to, Garrett couldn't help but peek at the labels, his own morbid curiosity overriding his desire to keep his eyes focused ahead or on the floor. To his relief, the products here appeared to be completely conventional. Baked beans, soups, jars of sauces. It was so... familiar. So much so that the horrors he had already seen could almost be forgotten as some kind of misunderstanding or a particularly vivid bad dream. Again, the ghostly vision of his pregnant wife appeared in Garrett's mind, and his thoughts turned to escape.

"Roughly how many people are in the store?" Garrett asked.

He suddenly felt very warm and was finding the urge to panic increasingly hard to resist.

"A few. Thirty maybe. I haven't really tried to count. We've been distracted as you can imagine," he added, giving Leena's hand a gentle squeeze.

"Okay, what about staff? Any idea how many of those there are?" Garrett pressed.

"Well, there are two girls running the checkout, then there's the manager, who I saw go into his office. There are a couple of guys stocking shelves, and the butcher up at the back of the store. Oh, and Lurch, the security guard over by the door. So seven in all."

Garrett nodded. He had seen the security guard when he walked in. He was a huge hulking eastern European-looking brute with a wide, flat nose, and eyes which didn't quite look head on.

'One eye going to the shops and the other on the way back with change,' his mother would have said, and he might—under more normal circumstances—have

laughed, if not for the other word that was bothering him more than any other Mark had said.

Butcher.

In a place that seemed to do a roaring trade in human flesh, the thought of being locked in with an on-site expert in the art of butchery didn't bear thinking about. He pushed the thought aside and turned to Mark, who had now removed the sunglasses and hooked them over the 'V' neck of his white t-shirt. He looked scared, and Garrett didn't blame him.

"Okay, that could work in our favour. We outnumber them, so we might be able to get some kind of plan together," he heard himself say.

"Thing is, not everyone is clued into what's happening here. It's not…"

Mark stopped speaking as they walked past one of the staff members who was busy re-stocking tins of baked beans from a steel-framed trolley. He was tall and harsh looking and tipped them a nod, his eyes cold as he watched them pass. They waited until they were a little further down the aisle, and then Mark continued.

"It's not all over the store, the crazy stuff. A lot of their stock is genuine. Like I said, designed to entice us to buy shit we don't need."

"Okay, so other than us, does anyone in here know what's happening?"

"Oh, I'm pretty sure there is, but people are either too scared to do anything about it, or they're trying to ignore what their eyes are telling them."

Garrett nodded. "Have you tried to talk to anyone about it apart from me?"

"Not really. I did try to talk to one guy, a big dude who looked as if he might be military. I thought his muscle might come in useful if we had to fight our way out of here."

"Where is he?"

"Over by the beer fridges at the other side of the store."

"Why isn't he with you?"

Mark shrugged his shoulders. "He was all for helping until he saw the human skin lampshades over in household. After that, he seemed to switch off completely. I think he would have made a run for it, but he saw what happened to the guy they took in the back, and I don't think he has the guts for it yet. He's been doing his best to get shit-faced ever since, just helping himself out of the cooler."

"Maybe we can help him? Both of us try to talk him around?"

"I don't think so," Mark said, shaking his head. "Best leave him be. I'm pretty sure the staff has noticed, and I don't think it will be too long until they take him."

"Take him?"

Mark licked his lips, and his Adam's apple bobbed up and down as he struggled to find the words.

"Out back," Leena whispered.

It was the first thing Garrett had heard her say since he met the pair. Garrett looked at her. Her eyes shone for a second, and he could almost feel the terror coming off her in waves.

"What's out back?" Garrett asked, already dreading the answer. Leena shrugged and returned to staring at the floor or her rainbow coloured flip-flops, or whatever it was she could see down there. Mark took over, letting Leena off the hook.

"There are some double swing doors up by the butcher's counter," he said, his eyes flicking from Garrett to Leena and back again. "My guess is they lead to storage or loading bays… or something. There were some kids in here earlier, just fucking around like kids do. Anyway, one of the staff came over to them, a broad guy with huge forearms and one of those stares that tell you he's not someone you want to screw around with.

Anyhow, the kids started to tease him. You know what kids are like, playing the big 'I am', especially when they are in groups of two or three like these were."

He nodded towards the entrance. "Lurch, over there by the door, came over and he and the stocky guy ushered them through those doors. We didn't see anything, but we were close by and we heard it. Good God, we heard it all." His voice wavered as he said it.

"What did you hear?" Garrett asked, not liking the glassy, faraway look in Mark's eyes.

"It was brittle and wet; the sound of tearing. I don't think I'll ever forget that sound."

His bottom lip began to tremble, and Garrett grabbed him by the wrist.

"Hey, take it easy, okay? Just relax. Did anyone else hear it?"

"I don't know, man, maybe. Even if they did, they probably did the same thing as the rest of us."

"What was that?"

"Nothing," he shrugged. "We ignored it. Walked away. As long as it's someone else's problem, who are we to interfere, right?" His lip began to tremble, and Garrett released his grip as they approached the bottom of the store.

"You understand, don't you, man?"

"Yeah, I get it," Garrett said, trying to think of something positive to say.

"I would have helped, truly I would have, but look at me, I'm no superman."

Garrett nodded. Mark had a point. He was thin to the point of being underweight. As far as any kind of physical confrontation went, he wouldn't be much help. A thought popped into Garrett's mind, one which almost made him laugh outright.

Not much meat on him. Might as well set him free.

He almost said it, yet somehow managed to turn it into a subtle cough.

"Come on, let's move on," he said instead as they entered the next aisle. As they turned the corner, Garrett discreetly looked at the checkouts and the two Slovak girls who sat disinterested at their empty tills. They were pale, with listless eyes ringed with too much thick black makeup. One of them was filing her black painted nails, the other browsing a glossy fashion magazine. They certainly didn't look to be a threat should an escape be on the cards. His eyes lingered a little longer on the automatic doors behind them and the blessed freedom beyond. He would most likely have tried for it, if not for the hulking security guard that was lingering with intent and watching the store with unwavering sharpness by the side of the door. Mark called him Lurch, and to Garrett, that was a pretty good description. He was absolutely enormous. Garrett suspected he was somewhere close to seven feet tall. His white shirt struggled to contain muscles on top of muscles. Giant, hairy forearms flexed as he folded his arms and watched. He locked eyes with Garrett for a split second as the trio rounded the corner, putting the tantalising freedom and the icy glare of Lurch behind them.

Garrett was looking at the dizzying selection of pasta, glad to see something normal when Leena began to whimper. Mark put an arm around her shoulder and ushered her on past the table which had been set up halfway down the row.

FREE SAMPLES! PLEASE TAKE ONE! proclaimed the hand-written sign pinned to the edge of the tabletop. On the table was a large white plate. It took Garrett a moment to understand exactly what he was looking at as it initially didn't compute. At first, he thought it was some kind of exotic new snack, but as the pieces fell into place, it became apparent he was looking at something almost beyond his capacity to absorb.

The plate was filled with skewered human tongues. Garrett felt his gag reflex spring to life as he cast his eyes over the macabre offering. Fat, black houseflies darted and buzzed around the plate, and Garrett could see that some of the tongues were covered in a pulsing carpet of maggots. A stack of napkins had been thoughtfully arranged on the table beside the plate.

Garrett moved his own tongue, just because he could. It suddenly dawned on him he was in a very real, very dangerous situation and his life was in danger. It was an incredibly sobering experience, one which wasn't entirely welcome. He moved on, waving away the flies looking for a good spot to lay their eggs. With some effort, he managed to walk past the table, forcing his eyes to look straight ahead and his nose and ears to ignore the horrid stench and angry drone of the flies. He caught up to Mark and Leena, and they walked on. None of them felt the need to speak. There were no real words that seemed appropriate, each of them content to deal with the horror in the best way they could.

It was Garrett who broke the silence as they moved away from the samples.

"We need to contact the police."

"I wish we could. We've been trying since we got in here."

"Yeah, you already told me."

"They must be blocking it somehow," Mark replied, draping an arm around Leena's shoulders and pulling her close to him.

"It would be easy enough to do. You can order a signal jammer on the internet easily enough. You never know what kind of range it might have."

Trying to remain as casual as he could, Garrett took out his own phone and was dismayed to see he still had no signal. He tried to call the police anyway, and when that failed, he tried to call Stacey. After trying three or four times to get through, he eventually gave up and shoved the useless handset back into his jeans' pocket. The argument which had triggered him to walk out on her to get some air now seemed less than trivial.

"Is she okay?" Garrett said, nodding towards Leena.

"Yeah, she's fine. It's just a bit of a shock to her system, that's all."

"Tell me about it."

"So we can't get out, and we can't get a signal to call anyone. What do we do now?"

"Now it's down to us and whoever else we can get onboard."

They turned into the magazine aisle, grateful to be away from the mixture of horrific delicacies amid the normality. There were two shoppers reading magazines which they probably had no intention of buying. The one nearest to the trio looked to be some kind of business executive. He was wearing a charcoal suit and brown overcoat and had skin which was a sore looking reddish-pink from a recent suntan. His nose was buried in a copy of *Time* magazine, and his briefcase and umbrella were clasped between his feet like an obedient dog.

The second browser was a little further down the aisle and sported a black t-shirt with a garish print of a werewolf on the front. Even from a distance, Garrett could tell he was the typical teenage loner. Not one of the cool kids who acted all broody as some kind of fashion statement, but a genuine geek. Nerd. Whatever you wanted to call him. The clues were many. The clunky unbranded trainers, the facial hair somewhere in limbo between designer stubble and scruffy hobo, and his choice of magazine—pro wrestling—finished the look. Garrett leaned close to Mark, still speaking in a whisper.

"We need to let these people know what we're up against. If we want to get out of here, we need to group together."

"We can't do that. The staff will know something's wrong if we start walking around in a mob."

"You might be right, but if what you said about this place enticing us in like flies, we're dead anyway. Either way, we need to do something."

"Maybe we can do it without being so obvious," Mark said as he paused to leaf through a movie magazine, just to keep everything looking natural.

"How do you mean?" Garrett asked as he joined him, his eyes staring through the glossy photographs and sensationalist words within the pages.

"Well, the way I see it, there's no sense in us swamping people with information and coming across like a pair of lunatics. As I said earlier, I'm pretty sure most of them already know what happened here. They should be easy enough to get on side. The problem will be those who are either in denial or refuse to believe it."

"Okay, that makes sense. So what do you suggest?"

"The Scooby Doo method."

"Say again?" Garrett asked, genuinely puzzled.

"Let's split up and go at this individually. It will look a hell of a lot less like we are pulling some kind of prank, which is my main concern. At least as individuals, these people will have to take us at face value."

"Okay, I can go with that idea."

"I'll take the geek; you talk to the suit over there. We can take alternate aisles. I'll do the next one over, and you skip on and do the one after that. When you hit the top of the store, you'll be in the clothing department. I'll meet you up there, and we can see where we stand."

"Sounds good to me. Let's do it," Garrett said as he started to walk away.

"Hey, man."

Garrett turned and looked at Mark, a terrified kid who, just like him, ended up in the wrong place at the wrong time.

"Yeah?"

"Be careful."

"Same to you."

Mark nodded and walked towards the pro wrestling loving nerd. Garrett watched him for a moment, still unsure how to figure him out. The crushing claustrophobia of being locked in the store threatened to overcome him, so he forced himself into action. Hoping that somewhere amongst the shoppers in the store, there was someone who could take charge and get them out of the mess they had inadvertently walked into.

CURIOSITY & THE CAT

Silas was starting to think something was wrong. He gripped the steering wheel, staring at the slab of inviting yellow light which spilled out onto the pavement. His friend should have been back by now, and he was starting to get the itch to run. He glanced at the rearview mirror, first staring at his own eyes then at the rosary beads hanging from plastic. Brought up by a religious family in Mississippi, Silas had always been expected to become a good citizen and follow in the footsteps of his family.

Certainly, his father had been a good man, a hard worker who did everything he could for his family. His mother was the disciplinarian, ruling the house with an iron fist. Still, despite the strict upbringing, something in Silas just couldn't get used to living like everyone else. He never saw the point of working a dead end job and struggling to make ends meet, especially when there was a world full of gullible people and easy money to be made. It was at this time, as a wiry fourteen year old that he had decided to become a career criminal. Unlike many who found themselves mixed up in crime, he didn't need to do it. He had money. He had a home. He also had an insatiable urge to see how far he could go, how much he could push the envelope without getting caught. People looked at him and saw a black guy, and assumed the worst. The truth was he was an educated man. He had enough qualifications to get a good job which paid well, and yet it never appealed to him. The idea of joining the rat race and becoming a slave to the machine horrified him. No. He would much rather live this way. Taking risks, savouring the thrill of getting away with it.

He stared at the entrance to the supermarket again and ran a hand through his hair. For the last twenty years since he made the decision to go into his unique career choice, he had learned to rely on his instincts. And now, they were telling him to get the hell out of there. He checked his watch and found himself completely unable to make a decision either way. He reminded himself that situations like this were the reason he usually worked alone. He checked his watch, and the same question reverberated through his head again.

Why hasn't he come out yet?

Straight on the heels of that question, another followed, a slight variation of the first.

Why hasn't anyone come out of there?

Although it went against everything they had agreed to beforehand, his curiosity wouldn't be overcome. In fact, the more he thought about it, the more curious he was. He glanced again at the black rosary beads and crucifix which used to belong to his mother, then with a sigh, shut off the engine, climbed out of the car and started to cross the road towards the store.

BERNARD

Garrett managed to keep his expression neutral as he looked at the rag-tag collection of shoppers who had gathered in the clothing department. Mark walked towards him, and they shared a look which said they were both thinking the same thing.

It wasn't going to be enough to fight their way out.

"Is this it?" Garrett asked, hoping there would be more.

"Yeah, this is everyone."

Garrett made a quick count.

"I'm sure you said there were more people in the store than this?"

"There are, some didn't believe me, and some have just lost it."

Garrett nodded. He had seen a few himself as he tried in vain to get people to believe him. He half wondered if speaking to them and looking into their dead, haunted eyes was a glimpse into the future for them all.

"Yeah, I saw a few of those myself."

"Fuckin' awful to see, man. I think on some level they know what's going on, but something inside seems to have switched off. They're walking around like fucking zombies."

Garrett grimaced and turned his attention to the rest of the people who were milling around the clothing aisle. One of them caught his eye, a skinny, sour looking man with a flat nose, deep forehead, and a long cruel mouth. His attire—sharp black suit and tie—screamed lawyer or some other kind of pencil-pushing profession. The man caught Garrett's eye and strode purposefully towards him.

"What's going on here?" he bellowed, addressing Garrett. "Your friend here insisted I come with him, and now I want to know why."

"Are you telling me you don't know? I already told you," Mark interjected.

"I only came in here to pick up some God-damn pills for this headache. Somebody better start talking sense to me right now, because the things you said, young man, are distasteful, to say the least."

Garrett flicked his eyes towards Mark, who wasn't even attempting to hide his disdain.

"Whatever, man, suit yourself," he muttered.

"Look, please just calm down, and we will explain. It's vital you don't draw attention to us," Garrett said quietly.

The man snorted and shook his head.

"Attention? You do realise you have us all standing around doing nothing at the top of the God-damn store, don't you?"

Garrett flushed with both anger and annoyance at his own stupidity. Despite his belittling tone, the man was right.

"Mark, go see if you can spread people out. Tell them to look busy, but keep it casual."

"I'll try, but it was a hard enough sell getting them to believe me in the first place."

"If anyone gives you any trouble, show them the free samples."

Garrett was surprised at how easy the words came, and he saw a disturbed look flash up in Mark's eyes.

"Got it. I'll do my best," he said before walking away, dragging Leena in tow.

Garrett felt a light hand on his elbow, guiding him away from the group. The skinny businessman spoke quietly as he led the way.

"Look Mr..."

"Garrett."

"Look, Mr. Garrett. I think we both know what's going on here."

"Yeah? Speak for yourself," Garrett grumbled, looking the man in the eye.

"Come on, isn't it obvious? That kid is obviously on something. Kids these days are on all kinds of drugs. However, you, you at least seem sensible. So please, man to man, tell me why you are going along with this deception?"

Garrett disliked the man. He was normally not one to judge and was a firm believer in giving people a fair chance, but everything about him from his overpriced suit to his patronising tone was rubbing him up the wrong way. Worse than that, he could already sense the man could—given the chance— stir up trouble. Garrett lowered his voice and turned away from the crowd.

"Do you have a name?"

"Winthorpe. Bernard Winthorpe."

Garrett nodded. The name fit like a glove.

"Look, Mr. Winthorpe, here's the deal. Something is going on here, and in truth, I'm still having trouble believing it myself. But I need you to keep calm and most of all help me to get the rest of these people onside."

"Onside with what? You still haven't told me what's going on."

"You really haven't seen it, have you?"

"Seen what?" Bernard hissed.

"This place, what it really is underneath."

"This is preposterous and I think I have heard enough. I'm leaving."

Bernard turned to leave, and before he could stop himself, Garrett grabbed him by the elbow and spun him around.

"Listen—"

"GET YOUR HANDS OFF ME!" barked Bernard, a flush of colour rising up into his cheeks.

Garrett looked at the milling crowd, who was now watching the pair with nervous interest. Garrett released his grip, and Bernard smoothed down his suit.

"Look, I don't know what your problem is, but you need to get a grip—"

"No, *you* need to get a grip. You and that kid are obviously trying to play some kind of joke. Well, find some other scapegoat because I won't play along with it."

"Just look around you, for God's sake."

"No," Bernard said, shaking his head defiantly. "I won't play along with these games. I won't be part of the joke."

A flash of anger raged through Garrett. He could feel his hands shaking, and had to ball them into fists to stop himself from lashing out and hitting Bernard in the face.

"All right," he hissed, "If you don't want to listen to me, then don't listen to me. Go see for yourself. Check the meat aisle. Even better, check the special freebies in aisle four."

Bernard grinned an ocean of white against his cocoa skin.

"Oh, you'd like that, wouldn't you? Well, your joke-shop props won't work on me. This isn't the God-damn movies. By all means, you go ahead and do whatever it is that you feel the need to do, just leave me alone."

Bernard made to leave, and for the second time, Garrett grabbed him by the arm and stopped him.

"So you do know? You've seen what's going on here?"

"If you mean the rubber feet and pickled baby props, then yes. I've seen them. And frankly, I'm not impressed. This joke is in incredibly poor taste," he shot back, pulling his arm free.

Garrett saw it in him then. Saw that behind the defiance and the blind anger, Bernard was as frightened as the rest of them. He just hadn't figured out a way to deal with it yet. Hoping to diffuse the situation before it escalated out of control, Garrett lowered his voice.

"Look, I know this situation is messed up. Hell, I'm having trouble dealing with it myself. Either way, what's happening here is real, and like it or not we need to deal with it."

"Do what you want as long as you keep me out of it."

Despite knowing Bernard was just a man afraid, Garrett's dislike for him didn't dissipate. If anything, it grew. He leaned close and grinned, wondering if it looked as insane on the outside as it felt as it stretched across his face.

"Okay, point taken," he whispered. "You don't believe any of this at all. I get it. If that's the case, then you wouldn't mind doing me a favour."

"I hardly think—"

"My car is parked out front. It's a red Toyota pickup. I'd like you to go outside and grab my spare phone from the passenger seat."

"This is ridiculo—"

"Don't bring it in here," Garrett continued, not letting Bernard get a word in. "Nobody can seem to get a signal inside the building. When you're out there, call the police. Tell them to send everything they have down here to help us because even if you can't or won't see it, we are all in a dire situation. I'd go so far as to say we're in the shit up to our necks, maybe even higher. So, what do you say, Bernard? You fancy giving it a go?"

Garrett stood tall and held his car keys out to Bernard, horrified to find the sick grin wouldn't fade.

"No, I'm not ready to go yet."

Garrett could see a light sweat forming on Bernard's brow, and even though he knew he was being cruel, he couldn't help turning the screw a little more.

"Come on, Bernie, what is there to be afraid of? This is a big prank, after all, remember? Yep. Me and all of these other people were so intent on playing a prank on you— a man I've never met and would have nothing whatsoever to gain from fooling— that we rented out an entire supermarket, which we staffed and then filled with severed body parts, all in the name of comedy. How about you get your head out of your own ass and pay attention to what's going on here?"

"You're as deluded as the kid. You ought to know better!"

"Forget the denial, and actually, look at what's going on around you."

"I refuse to be drawn into this fantasy of yours," growled Bernard.

"Then step outside and make that call for me."

Bernard grinned, his face twisting into a sneer.

"Do your own errands. I won't do it."

"Why?"

"I don't have to justify myself to you."

"Because you know you will never make it."

The two men were now nose-to-nose, Garrett smiling, Bernard wide-eyed and glaring.

"Do it yourself. Just leave me alone," Bernard whispered, and walked away, melting back into the group.

Garrett walked in the opposite direction, ignoring the questioning eyes of the people who seemed to be looking to him as if he had the answer to their collective problem. Mark was standing with the old couple Garrett had seen when he first entered the supermarket.

"I take it that didn't go well?" Mark said with a nervous grin as Garrett approached.

"You could say that."

"Are you okay, son?" the old woman said, smiling warmly.

"I'm fine, thank you."

"This is Mr. and Mrs. Harwell," said Mark, who still couldn't quite manage to distinguish grimace from smile.

The old man held out his hand and Garrett shook it.

"Mark here has filled us in on the situation," the old man said, subconsciously putting an arm around his wife's shoulders. "This seems to be quite the situation."

Despite his age (which Garrett put at seventy or so) the old man seemed sharp. His hair was white and wispy like cotton, and he wore his sideburns in long lamb chops down his cheeks. His eyes were the colour of lead, and his face was set in a determined grimace. His wife was shorter and a little overweight. She wore a red head scarf and wore the same frightened expression as many of those waiting to be told what to do.

"Donald and I didn't even see the...objects in the refrigerators. We're both vegetarians," she said softly as she wrung her hands.

"How are you both coping?" Garrett asked.

"Okay, under the circumstances," Donald muttered. "Any idea what we do now?"

"I'm not sure yet."

"It's looking pretty bleak, isn't it, son?"

Garrett nodded as he felt his stomach plummet into his shoes.

"So what did the suit have to say?" Mark asked, hoping to break the tension.

"He's in denial. Thinks this is all a big hoax designed to make him look stupid."

"Why is he still here then?" Mark responded, glaring toward Bernard, who was standing on his own and checking his phone for signal, with the same success rate as everyone else.

"I asked him to go out to my car and grab my phone since he thought it was all bull, but he wouldn't do it. I think part of him knows what's going on here; he's just not quite willing to accept it."

"Want me to try it, son?" Donald asked, looking Garrett in the eye.

"No, I wouldn't ask you to do that. Hell, even though Bernard is a dick, I wouldn't have let *him* go through with it. I just wanted to see if he would."

"So what do we do now?" Donald asked, and Garrett found all eyes were on him. He was about to admit he had no clue when Mark spoke.

"Hey, check it out."

They all turned to look in the direction Mark had nodded.

One of the other customers— the businessman in the brown overcoat that had been in the magazine aisle— was heading to the checkout with his magazine. Arsenio was his name, and Garrett had tried without success to convince him to join the rest of the people at the back of the store. He had outright refused despite Garrett patiently explaining the gravity of their situation. For a time Arsenio had responded with grunts or nods, then eventually stopped responding at all and stared at the words in his magazine as if Garrett didn't exist. Frustrated, Garrett had left him to his own devices and now watched along with the rest of the group as he approached the checkout.

One of the checkout girls put down her nail polish and took his magazine, scanning and placing it into a red branded Grueber's bag. Garrett could see them engaged in conversation, a little lighthearted banter. The girl laughed at something Arsenio had said then gave him his change. It looked for all the world like a regular transaction. No monsters, no things that go bump in the night. Garrett flicked his eyes towards Bernard and was surprised to find his gaze met. Bernard had a look on his face, an arrogant sneer which said, '*I told you so, you dumb shit.*'

Garrett looked away and exhaled, not realising he had been holding his breath. They all watched as Arsenio slipped through the checkout and walked towards the door. For a split second, it crossed Garrett's mind they might, in fact, have all been wrong, and walking out was an option after all. No sooner had the thought presented itself than everything seemed to happen.

Arsenio was almost free and clear when the mountain of a security guard stepped forward and held out a hand. He and Arsenio engaged in conversation for a moment. Arsenio tried to push the security guard's hand away and held up his receipt. The guard— the one earlier (and accurately) referred to as Lurch, shook his head and spoke into his radio attached to the shoulder of his white shirt. Arsenio pointed over to the girl at the checkout, but she was paying no attention, too busy repainting her nails for the tenth time as she waited for her next customer to even acknowledge the commotion.

Whilst Arsenio pleaded his case, two men came out of one of the office doors and casually approached the pair. Garrett saw them coming and stepped forward to go and help when he felt light fingers on his arm.

"Don't do it, son," Mrs. Harwell said, her round face ashen and eyes dark with fear as she watched the scene unfold. "I think it's too late for anyone to help him now."

Garrett nodded, and feeling like some kind of awful voyeur, turned back to watch.

The two men who had come from the office were now standing at either side of Arsenio, boxing him in. All four men were engaged in what looked to be an intense conversation which wasn't quite loud enough to be heard from the back of the store. Garrett took the opportunity to assess the men who had come out of the office. The taller of the two exhibited all the hallmarks of the store manager. He was wafer thin. Some might say undernourished His hair was black and slicked back against his head and even observed from a distance, he carried the unmistakable air of arrogant authority. He nodded patiently as Arsenio spoke, gesticulating and again pointing to his receipt. The manager's colleague was shorter, but broad across the chest. He simply stood with his arms folded and watched everything unfold with a glare which was two parts intimidating, one part amused. Arsenio shook his head, tossed the magazine down and tried to shove his way past Lurch towards the exit. The stocky man grabbed him roughly by the arm, twisting it behind his back. The store manager took Arsenio's other arm and whispered something in his ear before the duo led him away from the exit. A few of the people around Garrett murmured under their breath as they watched the man frog march Arsenio away from the freedom of the outside world towards a plain white door labelled ' employees only'.

"That's where they took the other guy," Mark whispered to nobody in particular.

It was car crash mentality. Some of those gathered looked away as Arsenio was led from the door, perhaps assuming there was nothing more to see. Others couldn't help but stare at the events as they unfolded. Garrett was in that second group. He had to see, had to know how it all played out. The manager plucked out a large bunch of keys from his belt and opened the door. He held it open just enough for his short companion to shove Arsenio over the threshold. Arsenio squirmed and tried to free himself, knocking the door with his shoulder and –just for a second- revealing what lay beyond the threshold. A terror even worse than the sight of the severed feet in the fridge raged through Garrett as he saw what lurked behind that innocuous white door. Instead of the office which Garrett would have expected to see, perhaps a table and chairs where Arsenio would be held until the police arrived to question him as to what happened, the room had far more sinister décor. The floor and walls were green tiles not unlike an operating theatre of some kind, and during his brief glimpse inside the room, Garrett saw the edge of what appeared to be a stainless steel autopsy bench. Arsenio saw what awaited him and began to struggle and twist away from his captors. Nauseous and unable to believe what was unfolding in front of his eyes, Garrett watched with sick fascination as the men ushered Arsenio over the threshold and closed the door, leaving the fate of their prisoner a mystery. Garrett's eye caught that of the taller man as he closed the door. The man smiled, and when he did, Garrett almost unleashed the scream that had been swimming around in his guts since he first saw the severed foot in the fridge.

SALLY & ELLIE

"What's happening? I can't see," Ellie Connell said, frowning at her mother who was ignoring her.

Ellie tried to look around the tangle of legs and torsos of the people gathered around the store, then gave up.

"Mom, answer me. What's going on?"

"Nothing, nothing at all," Sally replied, only half listening to her eight-year-old daughter.

"This is a crock of s-h-i-t," Ellie said, spelling out the word she knew she shouldn't say and folding her arms for emphasis.

"Eleanor Connell! You know better than that."

"It's not swearing if you spell it out," she replied with a cocksure grin.

Sally would have, under any other circumstances, punished her daughter; however, the current situation was far more pressing, if not frightening.

"You still can't swear, Ellie, even if you spell it out."

"That's not fair. It doesn't count."

"I say it does."

"Can we go home now?"

Sally looked at her daughter and somehow managed to hide her terror.

"Soon. We need to pick up a few more things first."

"Then why are we just standing around with all these people?"

Sally was struggling to formulate an answer, or at least a believable lie when Mark walked towards them, getting her off the hook, for the time being at least.

"How are we doing over here?" he said, managing to smile for Ellie's sake.

"Good, thanks," Ellie said, smiling back at Mark. He felt something in his chest give a little at the thought of a little girl being caught up in whatever was going on. A quick glance to Sally said she felt the same.

"Glad to hear it," he said, somehow keeping the game in progress. "How about you?" he said to Sally.

"Okay, I suppose. I…" She cleared her throat and looked lost for a moment. Mark was struck with how similar mother and daughter were. Same light orange hair, same blue eyes and freckles. Even the same slightly miss shaped nose.

"What happens now?" she said, catching Mark off guard.

"Well, I'm not sure."

"You asked us to come back here with you, and it's obvious by now something's happening. I assumed when you gathered us together you had some kind of plan."

"Sorry, we're working on it."

"Yeah, I saw you with that other guy," she replied, looking past him to Garrett. "Between you and me, he doesn't look so good."

Mark glanced over his shoulder and saw that Garrett was indeed walking around with a dreamy and vacant expression on his face which did little to boost his confidence.

"He's a good guy. I think he's just struggling with what's happening here."

"And what is happening here?" she asked, eyes searching him for a definitive answer.

Mark glanced at Leena, then discreetly nodded towards Ellie.

"Hey," Leena said, just about forcing a smile. "Why don't we go see if we can find a magazine or something to read?"

"Can I?" Ellie asked her mother, still painfully unaware of the dire situation they were in.

"Of course, as long as you stay in the magazine aisle and with…"

"Leena."

"...Leena and do as she says. Got it?"

"Yeah, I got it."

"Okay, go on then."

Ellie took Leena's outstretched hand and the two made for the magazine aisle. As soon as she was out of sight, the two dropped the pretence all was well, and let the true horror they felt come to the surface.

"I need to get my daughter out of here," she said as she watched her disappear into the milling crowd.

"We all need to get out of here."

"I hope you have something in mind. There are...things on the shelves here that I really can't think about. I don't want my little girl to see them. There were brains..." She trailed off and produced a tissue, dabbing the corners of her eyes.

"Everything will be okay. We just need to stick together."

"I know you don't know me, and although this might seem unfair, I need to ask you something."

"Go ahead," Mark said.

"No matter what happens to me, I want you to promise to get my little girl out of here."

"I'll try my best."

"No, that's not good enough. I need you to promise me."

He could see how close she was to losing it, and noted how the same could be said for any one of them. He felt suddenly responsible for her, to ensure her and her daughter were safe.

"You have my word, I'll do everything I can to make sure both you and your daughter get out of here."

She wanted more, then perhaps realising she was asking too much already, nodded. "Okay, then I trust you. Is there anything I can do to help?"

Mark shook his head. "Not right now. Stick close to your daughter. Keep out of sight. As soon as we have a plan, I'll come and let you know."

"She's all I have, you know."

Mark nodded, wishing he had something else to tell her.

"I better go find out what's going on," he said, then went to look for Garrett.

MAKING PLANS

Shock was a funny thing, Garrett thought as he wandered aimlessly amid the racks of leisure wear. It was one of those terms that always seemed so throwaway in the movies.

'Oh my god, he's in shock,' some slick doctor would say about his patient after they had experienced some trauma during act one, which the TV star would duly fix after a few false leads and unexpected twists and turns just before the show ended. However, in reality— the reality that was the windowless building where they were now trapped— the shock was a very real, palpable thing. He walked amid the racks of clothes and felt somehow detached from his body. Everything was happening too fast, and none of it made any sense. For the first time, he was seriously considering the possibility he might never see Stacey again. He knew it was fruitless, yet he tried to call her again anyway, without success. He paused in front of a mirror, handily positioned to allow prospective purchasers to try on one

of the cheap shirts or hats before they bought them. He used it now to assess himself.

Hair, sandy and full, skin pallid, but that at least was understandable under the circumstances. He looked at his reflection with blue eyes which were filled with a haunting disbelief. His stubble—grown initially for fashion— now simply made him look old and tired. He had a lean, thin body, and dressed in his scruffy jeans and white t-shirt. He looked perfectly... average. He thought he looked like a man in his late thirties with a drug problem, when, in fact, he was only twenty-six and— apart from a few cheeky joints when he was a student— drug free. For the third time, he passed the suit trousers, looking but not really seeing, and thinking about everything and nothing at the same time. Mark approached his agitation hard to miss.

"Hey, man, how you holding up?" he asked.

"Not too good if I'm honest. How about everyone else?"

"Well, the little show with the guy who tried to leave seemed to have convinced most people there's something going on here."

"Bernard?" Garrett asked hopefully, unable to shake the sense of unease that overcame him whenever he thought about him. Mark shook his head.

"He's still having none of it. In fact, he's out there telling people it's all bullshit, trying to rally them together."

"Son of a bitch. We can't risk losing anyone else."

Garrett cast a wary eye towards Bernard, who was deep in conversation with a heavyset man with a huge, overhanging beer gut.

"Are you sure you are okay?"

Garrett opened his mouth with every intention of telling Mark all about what he saw as the manager ushered Arsenio away, but then remembered he was just a kid and was already struggling to cope. Instead, he coughed quietly into his hand.

"I'm okay I guess, I'm just thinking about my wife. I should have been home by now. She'll be worried."

"I know what you mean. I keep thinking the same, that we would have been fine if we hadn't stopped here. Hell, it was only a snap decision because I wanted a couple of beers for later... look at us now."

"How long have you two been a couple?"

"A couple of years. We've known each other since we were seven. We just kind of went from friends to more as we got older."

"How old are you?"

"Seventeen."

Garrett grimaced. It wasn't fair someone of such a young age should be dealing with a situation like this.

Mark looked Garrett in the eye and spoke in a near whisper.

"She's actually in a bad way. She's not coping at all. I gave her some sedatives to calm her down, but I doubt under the circumstances they will help her. I'm..."

He trailed off, staring at the floor.

"What is it?"

"I'm afraid she's losing it. I'm scared she's becoming one of them."

He nodded towards the zombie-like people who were aimlessly walking around the supermarket, eyes vacant and glassy, skin pale. Those people who, when faced with the horror unfolding around them, had just 'switched off' and were in some deep place within themselves where they wouldn't have to deal with what was happening.

"I think a lot of us will get like that if we don't manage to get out of here," Garrett replied as he scratched at his stubble.

"Any ideas?"

Garrett hesitated before he answered, then realised there was no easy way to say it.

"We might have to kill them if we want to get out of here."

He expected Mark to rebuff the idea, or to call him crazy and talk him out of it. Instead, he simply nodded.

"Okay."

"Okay?" Garrett repeated.

"If you think that's what's best."

"You don't seem so sure."

"It's a pretty big deal, man. Think about what we're talking about here."

"It's not as if it's a snap decision," Garrett said, making sure nobody could overhear them. "I've been thinking about it for a while, and as best I can see, it's the only way of getting out of here."

"There must be some other way, something less extreme."

"If you have any ideas, I'm happy to hear them."

"No, I know we might have to do this. It's just a big thing. I mean, resorting to killing people…That's a road we can't turn away from once we go down it."

"You seem reluctant and I can understand that. Trust me, all that matters to me is getting out of here. I'll do whatever it takes to make it happen."

"Me too. I mean, I just want to get Leena and me out of here alive, plus there's a kid here, I promised the mother I would help them."

"You shouldn't do that. We can't promise anything."

"I didn't intend to. It's just…she was desperate and I didn't know what to say."

"I get it. I wasn't trying to give you shit over it. We just need to be careful about giving people false hope."

"False hope? Don't you think we can get out of here alive?"

Garrett hesitated, which was enough.

"You don't do you?" Mark said.

"It's not that, it's just when I think about what we're dealing with. When I think about the things we've seen, it makes it hard to be positive."

"Well, we better get positive," Mark said. "Especially if you are thinking about going to the extremes in order to get out of here."

"I know, and I'm trying to. I get the impression you're not on board with this."

"It's not that," Mark said quietly. "As much as I can stand here and tell you I agree, I just don't know if I'll be able to go through with it when— if— the time comes."

"Neither do I," agreed Garrett. "Same goes for everyone else here I expect. But the fact is, we might have to if we want to survive."

"Whatever happens, we need more than just the two of us to get onboard and help us put some kind of plan together," Mark said, glancing around at the rest of the people who were now broken into smaller groups as they chatted in hushed tones.

"We'll also need some weapons, something to take the fight to them with."

Garrett nodded. "Okay, you take a walk and see what you can find that we might be able to use."

"I don't think there will be much."

"Me either, but just do what you can."

"What about you?"

"You mentioned a butcher when you gave me the rundown of the staff. I want to find out where he is." Garrett felt gooseflesh prickle on his arms as the words left his mouth.

"Is that wise, man?"

"Probably not, but I don't like not knowing where he is in all this."

"What about him?" Mark asked, nodding towards Bernard, who had now added more people to his group.

"The less he knows the better, for now at least. Let's do this and be discreet about it."

"We need to let the others know."

"I agree, just not until we know more ourselves."

"There's one thing I don't understand."

"What's that?" Garrett asked.

"Why us, why is it down to us?"

Mark was scared, and it was plain to see. Garrett felt an overwhelming urge to lie, if only to put the boy's mind at ease, but no suitable deception came to mind and so the truth— as ugly as it was— would have to do.

"We were the ones who gathered everyone together. I think even without realising, we volunteered ourselves to lead this... group or whatever the hell it is, right from the start. Like it or not, we've put our necks on the chopping block."

"Hey, Garrett, can I ask you something?"

Mark was unable to make eye contact and stared instead at the floor. Garrett didn't want to answer questions. Not out of cruelty or selfishness but purely because he wasn't sure he would have the answers Mark was looking for.

"Sure, go ahead."

"What do you think is happening here? I mean all this." Mark gestured around him, his face tight and pained.

"I mean, shit like this doesn't happen in real life. This is the kind of thing you read in books. But with books when you have had enough, you can fold the corner of the page over and put it down and carry on with your life. This kind of thing can't happen, can it? I mean not for real?"

"I won't pretend to know any more than you do. To be perfectly honest, I'm kind of going with the flow here. All I know is whatever this place is, whatever the intention of the staff, we're here, and we have to find a way to get out."

"Do you think we can save everyone?"

The hope in his voice was painfully optimistic, and Garrett didn't quite know how to say it without causing any more distress or upset than necessary.

"Honestly? No. But I like to hope we can at least get some of us out of here. Truth be known, I just want to get home to my wife and forget this place even exists."

"That's good enough for me. I'll go see what I can find just as soon as I check on Leena."

Mark broke away from Garrett, flashing Bernard a disgusted glare as he passed him. Garrett couldn't help but smile a little as he walked towards Mr. and Mrs. Harwell, who were sitting on a wooden bench pretending to try on shoes with the same 'going through the motions' mentality as Garrett himself had done earlier. They looked right together. It was the kind of life he imagined him and Stacey to have when they were older. He buried that train of thought completely, knowing how easy it would be to spiral into self-pity and depression if he thought too much about the wife he may never see again.

"Mr. Harwell—"

"–Donald, son. You can call me Donald."

Garrett nodded. "Could I have a quiet word?"

The older man could see the tension in Garrett's face, and stood without argument and followed. They moved to the far end of the store away from most of the other people.

"What can I do for you, son?"

Garrett looked around to make sure they were unobserved and was pleased to see nobody was paying them the slightest attention and were altogether more concerned with finding their own way to deal with the situation.

"That man, Bernard," Garrett said quietly.

"Oh, him? That son of a bitch has been stirring the pot, all right. You and the kid seem to be quite a popular topic."

"That's what I wanted to talk to you about. Now, you know what's going on here, right?"

"Actually, no, I don't," Donald said. "But I know enough to see things aren't looking too good for us right now."

"I know what you mean. Now Mark and I are looking at ways to get out of here, but he—"

Garrett nodded towards Bernard, who was still talking to his audience.

"—Worries me. If he turns enough people on to his way of thinking, we could be facing two problems instead of just one."

Donald rubbed the back of his neck, and to Garrett at that moment, he looked incredibly old and tired.

"What do you want me to do?"

"Nothing directly. Just sit close by and listen to him, find out what he's saying. More importantly, find out if the others are starting to believe his drivel."

"I can do that easily enough, son. Then what?"

"Nothing. Just keep me up to speed. I'll catch up with you when I get back."

"Back from where?"

Careful, Ray. You don't know how this guy might react.

He hesitated, perhaps a little too long, and then found the words he wasn't even sure he wanted to say.

"Mark said there's an on-site butcher in the store. For obvious reasons, I'd like to know exactly where he is and what he's doing."

A flash of fear appeared in Donald's eyes, and he subconsciously looked towards his wife.

"What do you intend to do?"

"Only what I have to."

"I take it from the tone in your voice you don't mean idle threats or anything quite so... pedestrian."

He found he *wanted* to tell Donald his plan. Something compelled him to trust the old man, and if something as monumental as his intentions towards the butcher didn't send him running and screaming for Garrett's head, then there was perhaps one more person in the store he could rely on.

Here we go, Ray. Cards on the table.

"No. In this case, I think it needs to be a more... permanent solution."

Not for the first time, Garrett was surprised at just how calm the words sounded when he said them and wondered if it was a sign of being on the first step towards insanity.

"Son, have you thought this through? What you're suggesting isn't something to be taken lightly."

Garrett felt his face twist into a smile which felt as awful to him as it must have looked.

"That's the thing. I don't think they're human at all."

He regretted the words as soon as he had said them, and was about to explain what he meant when the old man nodded in agreement.

"No, I don't suspect they are. I saw it too."

"Saw what?"

"The manager, when he took that man into the room down there. I saw his face when he grinned at you. I wish to God I hadn't, but I did."

The image flashed up in Garrett's mind in sickening detail. The eyes. The teeth.

"You can't tell the others, not yet," whispered Garrett, checking over his shoulder to make sure they weren't overheard.

"I understand. That's exactly why I decided to keep quiet. The last thing we need is a stampede for the doors. The fewer people who know about this the better, but people are already on the verge of panic and if that happens, the slim odds we have are down to virtually zero."

"Agreed. We need to—"

Garrett was distracted by Mark, who was hurrying towards them. His eyes were wide, and his lips pursed tightly together.

"She's gone," he blurted, attracting a few nervous glances from the people milling around. Garrett and Donald exchanged worried looks.

"Hey, relax, okay? Calm down."

Garrett's words went unheard. Mark's eyes darted and flicked as he looked around him. Garrett thought he was just a half step away from that black, carefree oblivion that already affected so many.

"Leena's gone. I left her back there, and she's gone."

"Take a breath, son, and try to relax. Now she couldn't have gone far," Donald said, putting a reassuring hand on Mark's shoulder.

"Donald's right. She can't be too far away. Just calm down," Garrett added with no real confidence.

Mark did as he was asked, but Garrett still didn't like the way his eyes flicked, rolled and danced around in his skull.

"She might have just needed to stretch her legs and taken a walk," Donald said as he locked eyes with Garrett.

"She wouldn't go out there, not on her own." Mark's voice cracked as he spoke, and his eyes continued to loll and roll. "She was scared."

He's about to break.

Garrett knew it, and a morbid part of him *wanted* to see it, to watch how it happened perhaps in preparation for when it was his turn to make the transition from blind terror to never ending numb calm. Instead of observing, he heard himself speaking, his mouth going into business for itself and running on autopilot.

"Come on, let's go and find her."

Mark allowed himself to be led from the nervous, watching eyes of their fellow shoppers. As they moved away, Garrett looked at Donald, the old man's face stony and neutral.

"That thing I asked you to do for me…"

"Consider it done. You can count on me," the old man said.

"Thanks, I appreciate it. Just be careful. I don't like that guy."

"Son, you just go ahead and leave it to me. I'll find out what the idiot is rambling about."

Garrett nodded and set off with Mark to find Leena.

SILAS

He had walked past the automatic doors three times now, taking his time to look inside the store in order to try and gauge what was happening. He locked eyes with the Neanderthal security guard inside the door and averted his gaze, unwilling to draw attention to himself. The guard, however, had seen him and strolled towards the door, massive arms flexing as he spoke into the radio on the collar of his shirt. Silas ducked into the alley between the supermarket and the old laundromat which didn't look to have opened its doors for some years. Swallowed by the shadows, he immediately felt better knowing no employee on security guard money would risk following someone into the shadows, especially if they hadn't even done anything wrong. Silas waited and listened, expecting the hulk of a man to appear, his shadow foretelling his presence. Silas held his breath and waited, ready to run for it if he had to. Friend or no friend, self-preservation was his priority. Pushing himself further into the darkness, he strained his eyes on the entrance to the alleyway.

A crushed Starbucks cup skittered across the street chased by a few discarded food wrappers. Far off, beyond the steady hum of the air conditioning units on the outer wall of the store, he could hear the steady drone of traffic as tired office workers made their way home from another hard day in the rat race.

Silas took his phone out of his jacket, and punched in his friend's number, waiting for the line to connect. There was no dial tone, and he was kicked to voicemail. His gut stirred as the instinct to run grew a little stronger. It wasn't like Lee not to pick up, especially with his situation at home.

Something's wrong.

It wasn't the first time the thought had entered his head.

Maybe he was caught?

It would be a good explanation, although it didn't make sense. He was only going inside to check the place out. There would be no reason for anyone to detain him. Whatever had happened, he should have been out by now.

So should someone else. Anyone else.

That was most worrying of all. Nobody had exited the store. It was certainly not normal behaviour and only added to the list of things which were starting to worry him.

Silas took a step forward ready to leave the alleyway when something caught his eye. Further down the alley, past the boxes and dumpsters, a shaft of white moonlight illuminated part of the floor and loading area of the store.

There was blood on the floor.

A bitter taste crept into his throat as he looked closer. It looked almost black in the darkness, and yet, it was obvious what it was. A slick trail led from alleyway towards the loading door, and there on the corrugated roller shutter door was a single bloody handprint.

The very real possibility of something horrific and beyond words was happening inside Grueber's raced through Silas, and he was now unable to fight his self-preservation instincts. Lee would understand. He was sure he would have done the same if the situation was reversed. As much as the thought of involving the police went against everything he stood for, this was a completely unique situation. A quick anonymous call would at least aid both his conscience and his curiosity as to what was going on inside the supermarket. He started to jog towards the exit as he turned away from the bloody trail and ran face first into a wall.

No, not a wall. Into the immense chest of the security guard who now stood between him and freedom.

"I wasn't doing anything," Silas mumbled.

The security guard didn't respond in words. His smile said enough. He took a single step forward and joined Silas in the shadows.

He didn't even have time to scream.

BO

The first few aisles were empty apart from the ghoulish shells of people still walking their endless circuits of the store. Mark's earlier description of '*gone*' was as accurate as any. They looked without seeing, some still picking up random items as if on some level they were still compiling their weekly shop.

Others had gone deeper into themselves and simply walked in never-ending circuits. Garrett saw one middle-aged woman filling her cart with jars of pickled human eyes, the milky, floating orbs glaring sightlessly as they tumbled and bobbed in the murky liquid.

Another man in the next aisle had fouled himself. Even from some distance away; Garrett could smell his awful stench. Mark didn't seem to notice. He was half a step ahead, hurrying as fast as he dared without breaking into a run. He froze at the head of the pharmaceutical aisle, his eyes flicking hopefully to Garrett as he flashed a relieved grin.

Leena was in conversation with one of the staff. Her eyes were half lidded and heavy. She had several assorted packages of painkillers in her hands. Garrett's eyes went to the man she was speaking to.

He was short and greasy with narrow eyes and full cheeks. As he spoke to her, Garrett saw his teeth seemed too many and far too small for his mouth. He reminded Garrett of a villain from one of the James Bond movies. He couldn't remember the name. It was the one with the razor tipped bowler hat which he threw at his victims in order to decapitate them.

The portly little beast was listening intently as Leena spoke, his lecherous face contorted into a delighted grin. Mark tried to dart forward, but Garrett put a hand on his shoulder.

"Easy, keep it casual. Remember where we are and what happens here."

Mark paused and took a deep breath as Garrett led them towards Leena.

"Good evening, sir," said the too-many-toothed man in broken English.

Garrett nodded. Mark remained silent.

"The young lady just ask which pills were to make sleep."

Odd-job.

That was the name of the character from the Bond films this man was so reminiscent of, and as Garrett listened to him chew his way awkwardly around the English language, he couldn't help but feel a bristle of discomfort.

"It's okay," Garrett said, forcing himself to look the baby-toothed man in the eye. "We can take it from here."

"It no trouble, sir, we here to help."

Garrett looked down to the name badge on Odd-job's not-quite-white shirt. It was neatly embroidered under the logo— the same Grueber's logo in a swirling red font that had been plastered on the pre packed human feet— it read simply 'Bo'. Garrett thought it was apt that his name matched the slightly pungent smell that drifted from the unpleasant individual.

"Bo, is it?" Garrett asked, forcing himself to remain neutral as he pointed to the badge on his chest.

"Yessir," Bo said it all as one word and held out a fat, filthy nailed hand towards Garrett.

"Please to meet you," he said, still struggling to wrap his tongue around the native language. Garrett didn't want to shake his hand. He could just imagine how it would feel. It would be soft and sweaty. He couldn't help but look at his fingernails. They were overgrown and black with filth. Garrett wondered what kind of company would employ such a despicable little man in the first place, let alone allow him to mingle with the paying customers.

One that sells human flesh, of course!

He heard himself say it in his head and was suddenly sure he was about to burst into fits of giggles. He knew he couldn't let it happen, because if he did he didn't think he would ever stop. Instead, he went ahead and shook Bo's hand. It was just as he had expected—like shaking hands with a hot-water bottle. Mark put a comforting arm around Leena's shoulder and led her away, leaving Garrett and Bo alone.

"You no shop?" Bo asked, watching Garrett with eyes that were sharp and devious.

"I only need a couple of things. I can carry them easily enough," he said, wondering why he was even bothering to keep up the pretence he was anything else but a prisoner.

Bo nodded. He seemed disinterested in Garrett and was focusing all of his attention on the back of Leena's jeans as she was led away.

"What time does the store close?" Garrett asked loudly, trying to regain Bo's attention.

With what seemed to be a considerable effort, he managed to tear his eyes away from Leena's ass and back to Garrett.

"Oh, don' you worry about that, sir. We open very, very long time. We never close. Our customers like to stay long time in store, eh?" Bo smiled as the words oozed from his lips. Garrett went cold, and it took all of his determination to keep his voice even.

"Maybe I'll just forget the shopping and go home."

Bo grinned, his tiny, yellowed baby teeth framed by his plump, liver-like lips.

"I think sir might stay a while. Lots of good things to eat here."

Garrett didn't like the way Bo said those words. He liked even less the way he stared at Leena as he did it. His eyes devoured her greedily where she waited with Mark. Garrett felt a protective rage well up inside, which he somehow managed to control.

"Thanks for your help," he said as Bo again took a long, leering look at Leena.

"Welcome, sir. It nice to eet you."

Garrett was certain—almost certain— Bo had meant to say nice to *meet* you, and it was nothing more than a language barrier issue, but it still made him feel nauseous. The thought of that horrible, fat little man chewing on Garrett's flesh with his tiny mouthful of baby teeth repulsed him. He managed a weak smile at Bo, then turned away and made his way back to Leena and Mark.

"We need to hurry this along and get out of here," Garrett said under his breath.

"Agreed. Let's do it."

FAILED ESCAPE

Garret and Mark were in the home goods aisle. They had been walking in silence, and Garrett was surprised at how quickly his mind had managed to adjust itself to the horrors that presented themselves amid the regular goods. After a time, such gruesome things as lampshades made from human skin or ashtrays carved from upturned skullcaps became viewable without the reflexive gag or urge to scream. Of course, the items still horrified—after all, how could a person fail to be disturbed by such un-natural things. However, Garrett knew if he were to have any hope of survival, then he would have to push aside the repulsion of his surroundings and concentrate all of his efforts on escape.

At first, it seemed they would have a bounty of potential weaponry to aid them, but on closer inspection, the things they hoped would help— the kitchen knives and such— were plastic replicas and of no real practical use. So far, they only had a handful of wooden sweeping brushes. Garrett tossed a length of wire into the basket and continued to look for anything else that might come in useful.

"This isn't going to be enough," sighed Mark, now calm but also dejected.

"We have to try. We can't just give up. How's Leena?"

"I gave her some more sedatives. She's sleeping for now. Mrs. Harwell is keeping an eye on her.

"It might be for the best. The less anyone has to experience this, the better."

"Shit, Ray, you should have said something earlier, maybe we could have all taken a handful of pills and had a slumber party."

Garrett laughed, a sound that seemed to be from another lifetime.

"I have an idea," Mark said suddenly.

"Shoot."

"What if we rushed the doors, all of us, I mean? Surely, they couldn't stop all of us from escaping."

Garrett shook his head. "It would never happen. People might say they would go along with it, but they would never do it. It's just too risky."

"Then what do we do? We're gonna need more than brooms and wire to fight our way out of here. All this stuff is fucking useless."

"Maybe," agreed Garrett, looking in dismay at their pathetic potential arsenal. "Like it or not it's all we have. We're going to have to make the best of it."

"I just don't see how any of this can help us. I hate just hanging around here and waiting to see what happens."

"I hate it too. Right now we can't afford to rush into anything."

They walked without speaking, the pleasant tones of the easy listening supermarket music and the squeaking wheel of the trolley the only sounds as they scoured the shelves for anything that might help them.

"So, tell me about your life outside of here, Ray."

Garrett picked up a pack of mop heads and placed them in the basket, not quite sure how much use they would be and even less sure if he wanted to answer the question that had been asked.

"I'd rather not talk about it," he said reluctantly.

"Come on, man. Don't go all Clint Eastwood on me. Spill it."

Garrett grinned.

"I'm married. We're expecting our first baby in June."

"Shit, man."

"What?"

"I'm sorry, you don't need me dragging this up. I should have kept my mouth shut."

"Really, it's fine."

"I feel like a dick. I don't know if I should congratulate you or apologise for bringing it up."

"It's okay, you don't need to stress over it, we have bigger things to worry about," Garrett said as his brief smile faded away. "Besides, I've accepted the possibility I might never see the outside of this store again, but that doesn't mean I'm not going to do everything I can to fight."

"Well, that's something we agree on. So, what do you do? For work, I mean?"

"Why the sudden interest?"

"Sorry," Garrett said. "I'm just feeling the strain a little, and I'm not all that used to talking about myself."

Mark shrugged. "It's fine. I didn't mean to pry. I was just curious."

"It's okay, really. I don't mind talking about it."

"Fair enough. In that case, I'll ask you again. What is it you do for a living?" Mark said with a grin.

With the tension broken, Garrett found himself relaxing a little.

"I'm a school teacher."   "Bullshit you are."

"Why not?"

"No offence, but you don't *look* like a teacher to me. I mean, you look pretty…normal."

"Thanks… I think."

"No, man, don't get me wrong, all power to you. I'm just surprised, that's all. I had you down as a builder or an army guy. Hell, when I first saw you, I thought you might have been a cop."

"Interesting analysis, but wrong," Garrett said with a grin.

"So you ever lose it with one of your students? I don't think I would have the patience to teach."

"I teach preschool. Four and five year olds, mostly. They're a great bunch of kids."

Garrett smiled then felt it fade at the thought he might never see them again. Mark saw it and didn't pursue the point. They walked without speaking for a while.

"It's odd," Mark said eventually.

"What is?"

"This situation. I mean they *must* know we know about them, and yet they still haven't *done* anything to us. I... I just don't see the point of all this smoke and mirrors bullshit. I also think we need proof of their intentions before we start arming frightened people with weapons, no matter how flimsy they are."

"I see where you're coming from, but there is proof enough all around us. It's on the shelves, right under our damn noses. Nobody normal would be involved in something like this. And what about the people, the ones who were taken away? Aren't they proof enough?"

"I know; I get that," snapped Mark. "I just don't want this to blow up in our faces. However you butter it up, we are still talking about murder."

"I'd say it was more self-defense, but we're jumping the gun here. I'm still hoping we can intimidate our way out without having to resort to bloodshed. All I know is we can't just roll over and die and wait until they are ready to finish us off. Any other action by us, whatever it might be, will be the last resort."

"Look, I—"

Their conversation was cut off by a guttural scream which seemed impossibly loud and crisp in the otherwise quiet market. The pair abandoned their trolley of potential weaponry and ran to the end of the aisle, joining the other horrified shoppers in looking at the commotion.

The woman must have been an earlier visitor to the store. She stood by the open door marked *staff only* and was breathing in ragged, wheezing gasps. Her eyes were wild, and her blonde hair was matted to her head in a combination of sweat and blood. Garrett saw what everyone else did, but his troubled brain refused to believe what his eyes were showing him. She was naked, and where her left breast ought to have been was a mass of pulpy, raw flesh. A white shaft of rib could be seen poking out of the shredded mess that used to be her upper torso. The skin of her arm hung down over her hand like a half removed fleshy glove. The bloody woman broke into a loping, stumbling run, heading for the exit. She was quickly followed out of the room by the short, burly staff member who, along with the store manager, had earlier led Arsenio away. He too was naked, his plump body quivering and shaking as he hurried after her. There was so much blood. Garrett could never imagine the human body could hold so much. He couldn't help but notice how vibrant it was as it landed on the polished floor in great spatters. Garrett looked around at the myriad of pallid faces who stared at the girl and like him, they were unable to move. Even Bernard— Bernard who thought it was a prank and the entire thing had been done at his expense– was looking on and perhaps understanding the gravity of the situation for the first time.

She charged between the checkouts, and as she did so one of the girls lunged and grabbed at her hair, but the desperate escapee twisted free, the skin of her arm slapping against the checkout as she ran. The girl's pursuer had closed the distance between them and reached out a bloody hand to grab her. Just when it seemed as if her fate was sealed, he lost his footing on the bloody floor and crashed chest first into the edge of the checkout belt. The girl squirmed free and charged towards the door.

"She's gonna make it," Mark whispered, and Garrett couldn't disagree, as it was obvious that Lurch, the lumbering security guard, would surely not close the distance to her before she could escape.

It happened quickly.

Lurch moved with inhuman speed. Garrett didn't see him walk, not as such. He seemed to shift instantly from his initial position at the side of the door to the front of the girl within the blink of an eye. In one fluid motion, he grabbed her, his huge hand almost enveloping her head. Garrett watched, and for a few precious seconds didn't understand what he was seeing. Her body darted to the left and ran a few more steps towards the open door, then slowed and stopped. Lurch stood in situ, still holding her severed head in one hand. Her body staggered forward in one last reflexive step and fell to the floor then twitched once and was still.

The only sound was the steady pitter-pat of blood as it poured from the girl's severed neck and pooled around Lurch's feet. Everything seemed frozen in time. Garrett knew he couldn't hold on to it, this time, the horrified scream which had tried to present itself when he first saw the feet in the fridge, and the skewered tongues, and the manager's face—his true face behind his human mask— was coming. It was coming and there was nothing he could do to stop it. He opened his mouth, but someone— he thought it might have been Mrs. Harwell— beat him to it. She let out a horrified, high-pitched scream. It was like a trigger, a signal to let pandemonium begin. People scattered, charging aimlessly down the aisles, looking for a safe place to hide rather than a means to escape. Others stood in place, eyes wide, mouths open, still struggling to understand what was happening. Garrett felt himself dragged by the arm.

"Come on, man, this is our chance!" Mark blurted. Garrett couldn't move. He couldn't take his eyes from the girl's head, her blonde hair now a makeshift handle for Lurch, who was looking into her dead eyes with simple wonder. He felt himself slipping, going to that place where he wouldn't have to worry about anything ever again. Perhaps he too would now walk the aisles in blissful ignorance, waiting calmly for his turn to be dismembered and sold. He found he didn't mind, and didn't try to fight it. He would let it come. He would welcome it and allow himself to drift deeper and deeper to that safe haven away from all the horror.

Pain.

It brought the world—the real-world— back into stark focus. He blinked twice, his mouth hanging open in shock. Mark reared back and slapped him again.

"FUCKING WAKE UP!" he bellowed, shaking Garrett by the shoulders.

Although not quite together mentally, it was enough, and he found he was moving. He was just about aware enough to follow Mark, who grabbed Leena by the hand and was heading towards the back of the store. Around him, people screamed and sobbed and ran aimlessly. His cheeks stung and he could taste bitter blood in his mouth, but he didn't mind, because it was real. Because of it, he was aware enough to try to stay alive for at least a little longer.

"Where are we going?" Garrett blurted.

"Storage room! There must be a delivery entrance out back!" Mark panted as they skirted around a man still blissfully walking the aisles with that awful, haunting, glassy stare. Garrett wondered how deep into himself the man had gone to be able to ignore the chaos which surrounded him. He was envious. The large double doors loomed ahead. Garrett could see golden artificial light filtering through the small windows. They were almost upon them when the doors swung open, and Bo walked out holding a twin armful of dismembered human legs, apparently oblivious to the chaos.

"You cannot come ere, sir!" he squealed as the trio closed in on him. Mark couldn't stop his forward momentum and ran into Bo at full speed. In a surreal display, the severed limbs were scattered across the floor, and Garrett heard himself begin to laugh at the absurdity of it all. It sounded so much like a scream he doubted anyone would tell the difference. Mark skidded around on his back and crashed painfully into the wall beside the door. Bo stumbled but didn't fall. Garrett didn't slow, and in a single fluid motion, he reared back and swung a huge looping fist towards Bo. The impact was immense. Bo's head snapped back as Garrett's fist connected with his cheek and jaw. His legs buckled, and he crumbled to the ground. Garrett's momentum sent him crashing into the double swing doors, which burst inwards and sent him falling face first on the cold concrete beyond.

Hell.

That was his first thought as he scrambled to his knees and took in the panorama of the storage area. Countless human carcases hung from hooks— legs, arms, and heads removed and stacked neatly on benches ready for packaging. Arsenio—he who only wanted to buy the latest issue of Time magazine— now hung from one such hook, his eyes glassy and staring, his lower jaw missing. He had been hollowed out, his disembowelled body hanging obscenely from the hook and chain which were embedded into his back.

Hehasnolegshehasnolegshehasnolegs!!

The mantra repeated itself in Garrett's head, and indeed, it was true. Arsenio was absent from the waist down. Across the room was an old wooden butchery table stained with what looked to be a lifetime's worth of blood. The huge bear of a man standing behind it— all forearms and bad intentions. His slick head was spattered with blood. There was no mistake. He could only have been the butcher. He was busy de-jointing Arsenio's left leg, the lower half hanging at a nauseating angle. The butcher paused, the large cleaver still embedded in the knee joint.

"You can't come in here!" he bellowed, glaring at Garrett, who was now up to his knees and unable to do anything but stare. He scrambled to his feet and backpedalled, grabbing Leena, who was about to enter the room.

"Not in there," Garrett panted, pushing her back into the store. He grabbed Mark by the arm and yanked him to his feet, Garrett now leading the three of them towards the rear of the store.

"What do we do now?" Leena shrieked. Garrett had no answer. All he could see in his mind's eye was the butchery room and knew no matter how long his life would go on to last, those images would stay with him forever. The trio ran, weaving around the other shoppers who seemed as lost and aimless as they were.

"Try for the front door!" Mark panted. "Maybe we can slip out without them noticing."

It was as good an idea as any, thought Garrett as he changed direction, cutting at an angle towards the checkouts. The exit loomed ahead, and Garrett saw the guard— the one known only to them as Lurch. He was sitting cross-legged on the floor in front of the beheaded girl, his arm lost up to the elbow as he reached deeper into her stomach. He looked up at them as they charged past, offering a simple, childish smile. His face was streaked with blood, and as they watched, he pulled out an unidentifiable chunk of the girl's innards and scooped them into his mouth. The other staff members were indulged in similar acts.

The checkout girls were on all fours as they fed each other parts of an unfortunate shopper who hadn't been lucky enough to flee the chaos. His body was spread-eagled on the floor, his stomach open and exposed, a long slick of intestine looped by his side. The chubby chaser of the headless girl sat at one of the checkouts with her severed head in his hands. Garrett watched in horror as he bit her bottom lip away with a horrific wet tearing sound and began to eat it.

"The door isn't guarded. Come on!" Garrett barked, increasing his speed as he cut between two checkout lanes and towards tantalising freedom.

He ran. Ran like he had never run before. His pulse pounded in his temples, and his heart raced with the healthy thump of exertion. Nothing existed. There was just him and the door.

I'm going to make it, he thought to himself as a gentle, teasing puff of breeze drifted towards him from the doors which were less than fifteen feet away. He was almost upon them when the corrugated security grille slammed into place. Garrett ran into it anyway and rattled it, grabbing at the small holes in the metal and shaking it back and forth. He put his lips to the mesh, shouting through to the deserted street which was so cruelly close, eyeing his own car which was parked just a few feet away.

"Help us! Please help us!" he screamed, pounding the steel grille with his fists.

"Please, come back inside the store," said the smooth, calm voice to his right.

Garrett looked towards its origin, knowing who it would be before he saw him. The store manager offered Garrett a narrow smile as he removed the key from the security controls. Garrett stopped struggling and backed away, taking his place beside Mark and Leena, who had only just caught up. The store manager nodded. Garrett couldn't help but stare at him. His eyes had a depth and intensity that were truly terrifying.

"Thank you," he said curtly, then slipped the key into his trouser pocket and picked up the public address microphone.

"Ladies and gentlemen," he said politely, his voice amplified through the store.

The chaos continued.

"Ladies and gentlemen, please calm yourselves," he repeated, his thin smile wavering slightly.

"Oh, this won't do," he said apologetically to Garrett.

He reached out to a dial beside the handset and turned it to halfway. A piercing squeal emitted from the in store speaker systems. Garrett fell to his knees and covered his ears. It felt as if his brain were on fire. Around the store, the panicked shoppers fell to the ground almost as one. Only the staff and the ones who had retreated within themselves seemed oblivious. The manager smiled as he watched the people writhe in agony.

"Please," Garrett moaned through gritted teeth, "shut it down."

"Of course," said the manager curtly, and turned the dial back to zero.

The store was plunged into silence apart from the sloppy sounds of the staff gorging on the dead and a few isolated, frightened sobs.

"Now ladies and gentlemen, if you would be so kind as to remain calm and listen, I will explain what is happening here."

"Who are you?" groaned Garrett, the noise still buzzing angrily around inside his head. The manager with the hellish eyes smiled and straightened his tie.

CONFRONTATION

The remaining people—those who weren't dead or insane— were huddled in a tight, frightened group by the shuttered off entrance. The ones who had switched off altogether and were too far gone to acknowledge the latest turn of events continued to walk the aisles or stood and stared into oblivion. Garrett still envied them and their indifference. The store manager stood in front of them, flanked by the huge lumbering security guard and Bo, who had an ugly looking swelling under his right eye, and glared at Garrett through gritted teeth. A nervous murmur drifted through the throng of people as they awaited their fate.

"Ladies and gentlemen, if you would please listen closely," the manager said, holding his hands up in a calming gesture. "Allow me to introduce myself," he said, folding his long-fingered hands in front of him.

"My name is Alex Nicu, and I am the administrator of this facility."

Garrett didn't like the terminology. *Administrator* and *Facility* instead of *Manager* and *Store*. He flicked a concerned glance to Mark, but he was preoccupied with trying to calm Leena, who was deathly pale and trembling as he stroked her hair.

"I must apologise for the unfortunate...*event* you were just forced to witness. You have my assurance it was an isolated incident and was not a reflection on the rest of the staff here at Grueber's World of Food.

He offered a thin, pleasant smile which would have been acceptable if not for his eyes, which were still unreadable opaque pools.

"Why are you keeping us here?" asked a frightened woman from somewhere within the crowd. Nicu considered for a moment and continued.

"You wonderful people are incredibly fortunate. You have been chosen to become a part of something much larger and more significant than your individual or collective existences. Just by entering this facility, you have ensured that, for some of you at least, your lives will have a meaning and importance at a level far higher than anything you could have ever imagined."

Garrett leaned close to Mark and whispered, "Do you believe this shit?"

Mark didn't respond. He looked to Garrett like he was close to the edge of that increasingly inviting inner sanctum where sanity is lost forever and the troubles of the world are a problem someone else has to deal with.

"I will not lie to you, ladies and gentlemen," Nicu continued in his eastern European twang as his smile grew. "Some of you will not be leaving this building tonight. Some of you have to be sacrificed in order for us to survive. This is nothing to be frightened of. It is simply the way of the world. This is the way it has to be. Do not be tempted to fight it. This isn't a tide any of you, singularly or in any form of collective, can swim against. I tell you this outright in the interest of clarity. Out of respect for you as individuals. I would expect that same level of respect in return. There is no escaping this fate. There is no help forthcoming. I urge you to accept this situation, to embrace it."

A frightened murmur began to build.

"BUT—"

The people silenced.

"–we do not need all of you. If you do as we say and remain calm, many of you will be allowed to leave and return to your ordinary lives. The sacrifice of the few will save the many."

"And how will you choose?"

Garrett looked for the source of the voice. He thought it might have been Bernard, but he couldn't pick him out of the crowd. He either wasn't there or was keeping a low profile. Nicu smiled.

"We are not barbarians. Unlike your government, we will not try to inject our influence on any decision. We believe in fair treatment. It is because of this, we have decided to allow you to discuss amongst yourselves in order to choose who will be given the privilege of being sacrificed for our cause. To be chosen truly is a worthy honour. Something far greater and more important than your current existences filled with petty squabbles and greed for material possessions. Those of you lucky enough to be chosen will become gods of your people. Legends to be remembered for all eternity. But know this—"

Nicu's face grew serious, the smile fading as he held up a warning finger.

"There is no escape. No way out. The only way to leave is when we choose to release you. Any attempt to leave of your own accord will be punished severely and treated as an unnecessary act of aggression. Put simply, if you choose to do anything silly and cause a problem, those responsible will be dealt with in the most extreme way. There will be no mercy. No second chances. No excuses. If you do as we say, everything will go smoothly. If you don't…" He looked at the bloody corpse of the girl with the severed head, then turned his gaze to the crowd, ensuring they had received the message... "Do I make myself clear?"

There was no response. Part in fear and part in disbelief, the people watched and listened. Nicu paused, waiting for any objections. Satisfied there were none, he clapped his hands together.

"Very good," he said with a smile. "We require no more than ten of you. Please take as long as you need in order to decide who will be given to us. The rest of you will be set free. By all means, feel free to help yourselves to any food items in the store."

With a curt nod, Nicu walked smoothly to the door marked staff only, taking care to step over the bloody pools on the polished floor. He entered and closed the door softly behind him. Bo stayed just long enough to glare at Garrett before following, hurrying after Nicu like a well-trained pet. Everyone who remained looked at each other with frightened, disbelieving eyes, and Garrett was dismayed to find most eyes fell upon him. He looked to Mark for some support, but he and Leena too waited with expectancy. Only Bernard— making himself visible again now that the imminent danger had gone— showed apparent disinterest, and watched in half smug, half disgusted amusement.

"So what now?" he said, looking directly at Garrett.

"We discuss it and decide what's best."

"They already told us what the situation here is. We have to choose."

A few murmurs of agreement made Garrett more aware he was currently standing alone.

"Look, Bernard, I know we got off on the wrong foot, but if anything these events has justified why we gathered you together."

"Justified?" Bernard said with a smug grin. "You tried to make me go out there."

"That's not how it was. I—"

"He knew what was going on here, and he tried to send me outside."

Bernard was addressing the people around him, looking at them with the closest thing to puppy dog eyes as he could muster.

"I think he knows exactly what's going on here, and he's trying to keep himself safe and out of their hands."

A few more murmurs of agreement made Garrett squirm. He glanced at Mark again but was met with a neutral look of indifference.

"That's bullshit and you know it. I only called in to grab a few things for my wife. I'm no different to any of you."

"That's what he says," Bernard said to the crowd, pointing at Garrett as if he were some kind of criminal. "I for one don't believe him."

"You're being unfair. We need to stick together."

Bernard was on a roll now and began to walk around the rough circle that had formed. Garrett was again convinced he must be a lawyer or at least watched enough TV shows to have the act down to a fine art. Either way, he was good and was now smiling, the fear in his eyes not quite betraying his confident demeanour.

"Stick together you say, and yet earlier tonight, he asked me to go outside and retrieve a mobile phone from his car, knowing full well I would be killed if I tried. Isn't that right, Mr. Garrett?"

"You know that's not how it went. I was trying to make you see sense. Your head was so far up your own damn ass that I had to try something! I would never have let you go out there."

It sounded weak and Garrett knew it.

"You leave him be, ya' hear me. I was there, and that's not how it was," Donald said, pointing a finger at Bernard.

Garrett could have hugged the old man. Bernard glared at him and tried his best to intimidate, but Donald stood firm, meeting Bernard's gaze without wavering.

"This is no concern of yours, sir," Bernard said smoothly, trying to get back on track.

"Bullshit it isn't. This concerns us all, and standing here conducting some half assed witch hunt isn't going to help anyone."

All eyes were on Donald now, but he seemed less uncomfortable than Garrett. He looked unwaveringly at the crowd who stood around him.

"Donald…" Helen said softly, putting a hand on her husband's elbow.

"No, Honey, this arrogant ass is trying to pin the blame and I won't stand for it."

He whirled towards Mark and pointed a finger at him.

"What about you? You know how it went. You can vouch for him."

Mark lowered his gaze and then looked up into the faces of the expectant crowd, catching the eye of Sally and Ellie, their faces full of hope and innocence respectively. "Look, I don't care about who said what to who. I just want out of here, but yeah. He didn't know anything was wrong here when he came in. I was the first person to talk to him and point out what was in the fridges."

Bernard began a sarcastic slow clap; a wide lion's grin on his face.

"How convenient. His two friends vouch for him, and we're expected to buy it. I'm sorry, but I've been around for far too long to believe in such big coincidences."

"It does all seem a bit too convenient," said one of the men behind Bernard. He was wearing a checkered beanie hat and had a scruffy stubble beard.

"Are you serious?" Garrett said, feeling a fresh surge of anger. "I could say the same thing about you. Any of you. Maybe it was you people playing a prank on me. I wouldn't say anything so stupid as that, though."

"Why?" the scruffy man said, looking less sure of himself.

"Do you really have to ask?" Garrett said. Without letting the scruffy man reply, he snatched a package of dried human ears and tossed them to the man, who caught them instinctively. He unleashed a squeal which didn't seem to fit his personality and tossed the macabre package to the floor.

"Hey, there was no need for that, man," the scruffy guy said, his eyes darting between Bernard and Garrett.

"There was every need. Anyone who thinks this isn't a real and dangerous situation doesn't need to take my word for it. Just go look on the shelves and see for yourselves."

"He's making sense," the bearded man said to Bernard. "I mean, he's got a point, don't you think?"

"Don't be fooled by him," Bernard replied.

"I'm not taking sides here. What do you suggest?"

Bernard grinned, an expression more made from nerves than happiness, although Garrett was pretty sure he was enjoying every second of being in the limelight.

"I suggest we don't take any chances, and offer these three in exchange for our own freedom."

Under ordinary circumstances, the watching crowd would have laughed or ridiculed such a suggestion. These weren't ordinary circumstances, and instead, they watched. Watched and formulated opinions with almost matching neutral expressions. It dawned on him then that it didn't take much to make a crazy idea seem sane.

"Listen to yourself. Are you out of your fucking mind? You're suggesting murder!" Garrett blurted.

"He's got a point," the scruffy man said, now more agitated than ever.

"It's not murder. It's an offering. The sacrifice of a few in order to save the many. I believe in the military they call it collateral damage. And besides, it's no more than he tried to do to me earlier."

"You son of a bitch!" Garrett hissed and started towards Bernard, who took a cursory step back. Garrett was restrained, held back by a tall, long-haired biker with arms that were more ink than skin.

"Don't do it, fella," he whispered in Garrett's ear, his accent thick Irish, breath laced with the ashtray stench of a heavy smoker. "It's exactly what he wants."

Garrett knew the man was right and stopped struggling.

"See?" Bernard said calmly. "He would have attacked me. And you can be certain he would have marched me to that office and—"

Without warning, the biker whirled and punched Bernard hard in the face. He staggered back and crashed into a triangular display of boxed cereals, landing on his ass and holding his bloody nose as he stared at the immense biker in more shock than pain.

"You shut up now, ya hear? You open that mouth 'a yours again and see if you don't get another smack."

With Bernard now silenced, it seemed his spell was broken on the crowd, and they reverted back to their normal, if frightened, selves.

"Now we have all had a lot to take in, and I for one could do with some time to process it all," said the biker, taking his turn to address the crowd. "I suggest we all grab ourselves a bite to eat and just take a bit of time to think. Okay?"

A few murmured agreements followed, and then the circle broke, people heading away in different directions in groups or on their own. Bernard got to his feet, his suit now streaked with blood from his nose, which looked like it could well be broken. He glared at them in turn.

Mark.

Leena.

The Harwells.

The Biker.

Finally, Garrett. He said nothing, and simply stared with a smug smile on his face before turning on his heel and walking away.

"Fuckin' prick," the biker muttered under his breath.

Garrett turned towards him. He was six-five if he was an inch, and clad in the only kind of attire Garrett would have expected to see on a biker, black jeans and boots and a faded Sex Pistols T-Shirt with a sleeveless denim jacket over the top exposing his tattooed arms. His hair was black and long, and he wore long lamb chop sideburns. Despite his attire, his blue eyes were friendly.

"Name's Lee," said the biker, holding his hand out towards Garrett.

"Ray," he responded as they shook. "Thanks for stepping in there. I thought things were about to get messy."

"Ah, I wouldn't worry about him, fella. He's as afraid as the rest of us. He just don't know it yet."

"Well, I appreciate it all the same."

Lee nodded. "So, what ya think about our little friend's speech there?"

"I don't believe a word of it. That's about all I know for sure right now."

"It's deliberate," Donald chimed in. "They want us to bicker and fight and offer ourselves to them on a damn platter."

"But why? I mean, I don't get it," Mark asked quietly as he fidgeted from foot to foot.

"I see you found your voice at last," Garrett said with barely hidden anger.

"Look, I'm sorry, man. It's just… I don't know. That Bernard guy, he has a way with words."

"Yeah," Lee interjected. "I noticed that too. We need to keep an eye on him, that's for sure."

"You think he might be dangerous, son?" Donald asked. "I listened in on his little sermon earlier, and it did nothing for me. It sounded like crazy talk."

"Maybe, yeah. I think so."

"Is it something we need to… deal with?" Donald asked carefully.

Lee shook his head.

"If you mean what I think you mean, then the answer is no. At least not yet. We *do* need to keep an eye on him, though, and a bloody close one at that."

"I don't see how he can be a threat on his own," Garrett said.

Lee's expression changed, and Garrett saw how behind the bravado, he was just as afraid as everyone else.

"That's the problem," he said quietly. "He has a mouth on him and likes the sound of his own voice, and if it comes down to believing his rambling or becoming one of them—"

He nodded towards one of the mindless, broken minded shoppers still making their endless circuits around the store.

"— then people are apt to start listening. And *that*'s when we might have a major problem on our hands."

They stood in silence for a few seconds, the atmosphere heavy and oppressive.

"Well, I'm hungry. Anyone feel like finding a bite to eat?" Donald said, breaking the tension.

"I don't know about that, pal," Lee replied with a half-smile. "But I could use a beer."

The group began to make their way to the fridges at the back of the store as Bernard watched them venomously from a distance.

NO MORE FAVOURS

Garrett didn't think he would be able to eat. The thought of chewing and swallowing anything after what had happened repulsed him, yet not only could he eat, he was ravenous. He tucked into his second turkey sandwich— ensuring it was one of the prepackaged name brands he recognised— and thought about what to do. He looked around at the group— his group, or so it seemed. Like him, they seemed to have all found their appetites, and were sitting in small groups of two or three. Lee and Donald were drinking beer and chatting by the fridge, a completely unusual and unlikely pairing that somehow looked right all the same. Helen and the now awake Leena were sharing a large pack of Doritos and engaged in quiet conversation. Then, there was Mark. He wasn't eating or drinking. He was simply standing and staring into space. Garrett wondered just how far away he was from joining the ranks of the ones who were lost, and if he wasn't already part way there. Garrett set down his sandwich and walked over.

"Not eating?" he asked, trying to keep casual.

"I'm not hungry."

"You should eat something. You might need your strength later."

Mark looked at him then, and Garrett was shocked to see bitter anger on his face.

"What do you care anyway?"

"What do you mean? I thought we were in this together, all of us."

"So did I. But it didn't stop you from looking after yourself earlier and leaving us to… to whatever might happen."

"I have no idea what you are talking about," Garrett said with dismay.

Mark grinned, and Garrett wished he was wearing those oversized aviator glasses, because his eyes… his eyes said crazy, and in a situation like this, crazy could be infectious.

"Earlier," Mark blurted, glaring at Garrett, "when that woman came out of the office."

He paused, his Adam's apple bobbing as his eyes darted from side to side.

"You sprinted for the door like you were the only one who mattered. You left us to our own devices."

Garrett wanted to argue, to fight his corner, but when he recalled it, when he took the time to replay the entire sickening incident in his head, he realised Mark was right. Garrett had seen the chaos, and he had seen the open door leading to freedom, to his wife and unborn child— and he had run. Run and hoped he would be spared, no matter what happened to anyone else. Ashamed, he stared at his feet.

"I'm sorry, I... I just reacted."

"It's fine. I get it. Just don't play the hero card now that it suits you and expect me to like it."

"Hero card?" Garrett spat. "You think I *asked* for this? You think I know what to do? By all means, feel free to take the lead here if you think you know how to deal with this any better. You came to me earlier tonight; you might want to keep that in mind."

He looked around and saw the rest of the group was watching with interest. He lowered his voice.

"Look, I get it, okay? You're scared. And you're worried about Leena, but we're all in the same position. And despite everything that's happened, we need to stick together and get the hell out of here."

Mark smiled, but there was no humour in it.

"You know, I think that Bernard guy might be right. Maybe, there *is* more to you than it seems. Maybe you *are* out for number one and are just keeping us on side to help yourself."

"You came looking for me. You should keep that in mind."

"Maybe, maybe not. However you look at it, you showed us a side to you that you had kept hidden. You can't blame me for being a little bit pissed about it."

"I get it, and all I can do is apologise. I reacted. I wasn't thinking straight. Hell, is anyone?"

"You don't have to explain. Either way, I think we should just keep our distance."

Garrett knew then it was futile to argue. Mark had made up his mind, and it was obvious there would be no changing it.

"If that's how you feel, then that's up to you."

"It is," Mark said as he grabbed Leena by the hand, disturbing her mid conversation with Helen.

"The two of us will go our own way from now on. You do the same. Just to be absolutely clear, we're square. Even. No more favours, okay?"

"Mark—"

"Okay? Don't make this any more uncomfortable for any of us than it already is. I hope you get out of here, Ray. I really do, but I have to do things my own way now. I've made commitments to help people get out of here. I need to be able to trust people around me. I think for now I'm better alone."

There was nothing more to say. Garrett simply lowered his head and looked at the floor. Mark looked at the rest of the group in turn.

"Good luck," he said, then led Leena away. Garrett watched them go, trying to ignore the guilt that simmered in his stomach.

"Don't worry about it," Donald said, handing Garrett a beer.

"I let him down."

"Don't beat yourself up, son. The boy is scared that's all. He'll be back once he cools off."

"He's not the only one. I'm pretty terrified myself."

Donald nodded, and the two men drank in silence for a while.

"You know, Ray, sooner or later we're going to have to decide what we intend to do about this situation."

"I know, but how can we possibly make a decision like that? People's lives are at stake here. It's not something we can just decide on a whim."

"I know that, son, but if we don't, you can bet your ass he will."

Donald jabbed his thumb in the direction of Bernard, who despite his bloodied nose was still talking animatedly. Where there were only a couple of interested people before, he now had an audience of ten people hanging on his every word. Garrett felt a momentary flash of panic, although he wasn't sure why.

"I hoped that punch he took might have knocked some sense into him," Garrett said, taking a long drink of his beer. "If anything it's charged the son of a bitch up. He has barely paused for breath for half an hour now."

Donald smiled and took another swig of his beer. "He's a sharp one all right," the old man said, eyeing Bernard with contempt.

"What do you mean?"

"He has the same thing as my sister. The gift of the gab. The golden tongue. He talks, and people feel compelled to listen."

"Great," Garrett said as he watched Bo leave the door marked *staff only* and walk down the meat aisle. He was pleased to see that the bruise on his face had grown considerably.

Garrett saw the haze of fear and uncertainty that swirled inside the old man's eyes. He chose his words carefully.

"Thing is, Ray, if someone like him is left to talk for long enough, and people are desperate enough… well, I wouldn't like to think what could happen."

Garrett nodded and took another sip of his drink. It was crisp and cool, and he hoped it would take his mind at least temporarily off the gravity of the situation;

however, Donald was right, and he too found himself watching Bernard. He didn't like the way he was talking— calm but animated and…confident. He looked at the people around him. They were watching and occasionally nodding in agreement as Bernard launched into yet another enthused dialogue. Garrett wondered what the hell he was saying.

"We need to shut that son of a bitch up," Donald said, giving Bernard another cold stare.

"If either of us went anywhere near him, I can guarantee the bickering will flare up again."

"Yeah, I guess so. I would suggest someone else go and try, but I think our entire group is on his shit list."

Garrett nodded and then turned to face Donald.

"I'm going to speak to the manager. See if I can negotiate a deal."

"Ray, you do that and you may as well paint a damn target on your back. Killing yourself won't solve anything."

"I don't have any intention of killing myself. The truth is, I feel responsible and our options are limited."

"Still, I think it's better if we keep as far away from those…things who are in charge of this place as possible. I don't see any advantage to marching in there and potentially making things worse."

"Look, I know you don't agree with me, and I respect your honesty. Either way, my mind is made up and I intend to go ahead with this. I can't do it alone, though. I could really use your help."

Donald sighed and finished his beer. "Hell, for the record, I think it's insane, but I would never tell another man what to do with his life, so if you need my help you have it."

"I appreciate it."

"You might not when you get in there. Now, what did you have in mind?

PACT

"Will you come to help me find a new magazine?" Ellie said to Leena.

"Uh, yeah, of course, I will, Honey," Leena said, getting to her feet and stretching.

"Is that okay?" she said to Sally.

"As long as you don't mind, it's more than fine with me."

Leena slid her eyes to Mark then back to Sally.

"I won't be long," she said as Ellie grasped her hand.

"Come on, I want to get a good one," Ellie said, somehow still unharmed by everything which had unfolded.

"Take as long as you need," Sally said. Leena nodded. Unlike her daughter, Sally seemed to be struggling to keep a grip on her sanity. Her eyes were dull and devoid of all hope.

"We won't be long," Leena repeated as she was led by the hand by the anxious child.

"You okay?" Sally said to Mark as they watched them disappear out of sight.

"I'm fine."

"You don't seem fine."

"I'm just trying to figure out the best thing to do about this situation."

"I'm sure you'll figure it out. We're all relying on you."

"That's what I was thinking about. I really don't know how to get us out of here," he said, shaking his head and staring at the floor.

"You don't owe us anything, you know," Sally said quietly.

"I don't understand."

"I mean the stuff we talked about earlier. Things are different now. You don't have to feel responsible for me or my daughter."

"I told you, I'll get you out of here. I was always brought up to stick to my word."

"I'm sure you were," Sally said, forcing a smile. "You remind me of my eldest son. He's about your age. How old are you?"

"Seventeen."

"Oh, he's a little younger. He just turned fourteen."

"I *will* get you out of here."

"No, you won't," she said. Holding his gaze.

"What do you mean?"

"I know you want to, and I appreciate what you tried to do."

"And I still will."

"You can't make that promise," she said, reaching out and touching his hand. Her skin was cool, and even though it repulsed him, he imagined some of the packaged meats would have the same sensation against his skin.

"I won't give up on you."

"Things are different now. When we first talked… None of us could have known how things would turn out."

"You have to stay strong. They might not choose you or any of us, we might be okay."

Sally smiled and released his hand. "Do you really think they intend to let us go?"

"They said they would."

"They sell dead human beings."

He could only nod and avert his eyes. He was also starting to think none of them would ever see outside the store again, and had half an idea the promise of freedom was nothing more than a tool designed to keep them calm (or the meat fresh) until they were disposed of. It wasn't something he was ever willing to articulate until Sally had put it out there and ensured it would have to be dealt with.

"I know what happens here. But we have to try. We have to hope," he said, his voice close to cracking.

"There is no hope. All of us in here are already dead. We just don't know it yet."

"Don't say that. Think about Ellie."

"I am. I have. I don't want her to have to experience this."

"To me, that's every reason to keep strong. You have to fight," he said. "She's a strong kid."

"She's smart, too. She pretends to ignore what's happening, but I know different. I can see it on her face. She knows exactly what's happening here."

Mark chose not to answer, trying to figure out exactly where the conversation was going.

"If it gets to that point where we lose all hope. Will you take away her suffering?" she asked.

"What?"

"I don't want her to see any more of this. Every moment we are here, another piece of her childhood dies."

"Are you saying you would rather her be dead? You're her mother, you have a responsibility to protect her."

"Don't you think I know that?" she spat as tears rolled down her cheeks and streaked her makeup. "Do you have any idea how helpless I feel?"

"You can't just give up on her!"

"I don't want those things to cut her up and put her on the shelf!" she said, her voice breaking as the floodgates opened.

As horrified as the entire conversation made him feel, Mark could understand where she was coming from. He wasn't a parent, however, he could understand Sally not wanting to see her child displayed and sold. He couldn't believe the words were about to come out of his mouth even as he said them.

"Okay, if it gets to the point where there is no hope left, I'll do it. I'll do what you ask."

"You have to promise. I would do it myself, it's just…." Sally lowered her head.

Mark felt sick and realised with dismay this conversation and what he had been asked to do was more horrifying than even the awful things on the store shelves.

"How do you want me to do it? When…" He trailed off, unable to finish the sentence.

"When the time is right. When there's no hope left."

NICU

Twenty minutes had passed since Garrett and Donald's conversation. Even so, such a short space of time felt like a lifetime for those trapped inside the supermarket. People had started to form into small groups, pockets of two or three who stood around, watching nervously and waiting for something to happen. Others like Bernard tried to be proactive and continued to talk to anyone who would listen to what he had to say. He now had fourteen interested listeners to his seemingly never-ending sermon. For as much as the ordeal in the supermarket seemed to be draining the will from many who were trapped, for Bernard, it seemed to be energising him. Donald crossed the room, flashing Bernard a stony glare as he passed juggling two sandwiches, a beer and a can of soft drink in his arms. At seventy four, he was the most senior member of the group, and yet he didn't quite fit into the typical 'pensioner' stereotype. He had made sure over the years to look after himself, determined to do anything he could to keep father time at bay for a little longer. It dawned on him this was the first time he had truly been frightened in a long time, and had to go back to when he was a fresh-faced nineteen-year-old G.I in the army— something that at the time seemed like a fun thing to do instead of getting a real job, or at least it was until he was shipped off to Vietnam and experienced things so terrifying, so horrific it changed him forever. He discovered that war really was hell, so much so it didn't take long to make him a statistic.

He had been on patrol, walking through the intense, overbearing heat of the jungle with a platoon of fifteen other fresh-faced and frightened soldiers, all of them tense, all of them holding their breath whenever an animal moved in the undergrowth. It was during their third patrol since being sent over that they were ambushed, the jungle exploding in gunfire and the air filling with smoke as they scrambled for cover, not even sure where the enemy was It had all become real to him then, and he truly understood his life was very much in danger. He supposed he was one of the lucky ones. He was shot twice, once in the thigh and again in the shoulder, both clean wounds. Later, he was told by the doctor treating his injuries he should consider himself fortunate the bullet went straight through and out again without ricocheting off a bone and making mincemeat out of his innards or embedding itself in his brain.

His buddy, Johnny Grimes, a twenty-year-old kid from Ohio wasn't so lucky; he took one to the head. As Donald stood shaking and covered in Johnny's brains and fragments of his skull, he couldn't get the image cleared from his mind of the Polaroid picture of the pregnant wife Johnny had so proudly shown them not an hour earlier. You could tell he was proud that he was about to be a father. He brought it up in almost every conversation. As Donald had looked at the pulpy mess which was all that remained of his friend's head, he had made a promise to himself to get out of Nam alive and in one piece and to live a good, worthy life away from such horrors.

By the time he had been classed as fit to return to duty, the war was over anyway. Even so, he felt ashamed at the bitter irony that he had escaped with nothing worse than a slight limp, whereas poor Johnny's widow would have to face up to a life as a struggling single parent. He sometimes wondered what happened to her, wondered how she got on in life and what that kid of hers might be doing now. He hoped both had done well, and wished he'd looked them up before little by little he started to forget. In fact, he hadn't really thought about it for years until the horrors of the supermarket had made him drag up those old memories.

The rest of his life he lived as carefully and as risk free as possible. People thought of him as a soft touch, and because he was quiet and often preferred to watch a conversation unfold rather than take part in it, he was underestimated. Nobody knew that underneath the laid-back exterior was a man who had seen the worst side of the war and lived to tell the tale. It was later during his life, as old age finally reared its ugly head and started to onset him with aches and pains, that he was at a loss for something to do with his days, something to keep his brain stimulated and active.

He decided on a whim to join an amateur dramatics group. He knew from the start he was never going to trouble the Oscars or find he was some undiscovered natural talent, but he enjoyed it immensely and was competent enough to get by and take part in a few local theatre productions.

These were the skills he used now as he dropped the sandwiches and clutched at his chest, letting out a pained cry as he fell to his knees. All eyes were on him, and he knew this would have to be the performance of his life. He could hear Helen, his precious loving Helen, fretting as people circled him and assisted. He felt bad for not telling her, but making the entire thing as realistic as possible was the key. He writhed and gritted his teeth and allowed his eyes to roll back into his head. He could see the people only as ghostly figures through the top of his eyelids.

Away from the commotion and the circle of onlookers who had formed around Donald's distraction, Garrett walked quickly down the store towards the manager's office. He didn't look back and tried to keep his pace as casual and steady as he could. The nearer he got to the door, the more his stomach vaulted and tumbled. The chubby employee, the one who had earlier chased the girl to her death was standing outside. He was now dressed and had thankfully cleaned the blood from his hands and face. He watched Garrett with a cold blue stare.

"You can't come in here," he barked, holding a podgy hand out in front of him. Garrett saw he hadn't done such a thorough cleanup job as he had thought. He could still see the blood under his fingernails.

Come on, Ray, don't lose your nerve now.

With as much bravado and confidence as he could muster, he batted the hand aside.

"I want to talk to the organ grinder, not the monkey."

Anger and surprise flashed across the man's portly face and then was gone.

"Mr. Nicu is busy. He will not see you."

"I think he will. I want to talk about this little situation we have here."

"No. I am under strict orders that Mr. Nicu is not to be disturbed."

Garrett opened his mouth to speak when the door opened smoothly.

"Resoui, let the gentleman through," Nicu commanded.

Resoui complied at once and stepped aside. Garrett was now face to face with Alex Nicu. He was pale skinned and slender. He had a natural charm and elegance about him, even if up close he was much shorter than he had first appeared.

"Come in, Mr. Garrett," Nicu said, motioning to the office. Garrett tried not to think too much about how Nicu knew his name, or that he was about to lock himself in the room with some kind of…whatever Nicu was. The consensus was that they were cannibals, but Garrett was starting to think they were something else, something you only see in films or read about in books. The word beginning with 'V' and one he couldn't quite bring himself to say even though his pale-skinned host bore all the right hallmarks if folklore and Hollywood were to be believed. Too late to turn back, Garrett entered the office and Nicu closed the door softly behind him.

II

Back in the store, the rest of the shoppers stood and fussed around Donald, helping him to his seat and giving him small sips of water. Only Bernard wasn't involved. He had watched Garrett slip inside the door to Nicu's office and smiled to himself.

"Got you, you son of a bitch."

THE IMPOSSIBLE ULTIMATUM

Nicu's office was cold and smelled faintly of polish and leather. Nicu sat behind his imitation oak desk, watching Garrett, an amused semi-smile on his thin lips.

"Please, sit."

Garrett complied, and wondered, not for the first time, what the hell he was doing. He looked around the office, trying to gauge some sense of who Nicu was, but it was as pale and unreadable as the man himself. Eggshell coloured walls, indistinct green carpet, no photographs, or any other personal features. It was sterile and made Garrett immensely uncomfortable.

"I must apologise for Resoui. My son is impatient, to say the least."

Garrett was thrown off guard by how polite and articulate Nicu was. There was definite upper class sophistication about him. He nodded without responding, still trying to work out exactly who Alex Nicu was. It wasn't easy, as there wasn't a lot to go on. He would have put him somewhere in his mid to late thirties, and it was an age Nicu would have been able to pull off with ease if not for his eyes, which were a deep, almost opaque brown and looked to be filled with knowledge and a confidence beyond anything Garrett could ever hope to comprehend. Even without such an obvious name, Garrett would have guessed Nicu was Romany. He had the long hooked nose and high cheekbones typical of the race. Nicu smiled, and Garrett looked away and tried to make his scrutiny less obvious.

"I understand you must have many questions."

"I do."

"I must confess I find it curious the other people in the store respect you, for the most part, and yet… you come here in secret."

"Yes."

Garrett felt his skin grow cold as he watched Nicu hang on to every word that was said. It was as if Garrett was a unique creature Nicu had never seen before, and he appeared both amused and at the same time, almost overcome with a sense of childlike wonder.

"I assume you have come here to bargain for your collective freedom?"

"I thought that was the reason," Garrett said as he lowered his gaze. "In truth, I don't really know why I came here."

"Isn't it obvious? The people out there look to you for guidance. In such a situation, I'm sure you felt any action, however futile, was better than no action at all." Nicu smiled, and now he didn't look like a wonder-filled child. He looked like a lion toying with its prey.

"I don't know. I suppose so."

"May I ask you a question, Mr. Garrett?"

Garrett nodded. He didn't like the way Nicu was watching him. He leaned forward slightly and bore his ancient gaze right into Garrett's soul. He imagined he could feel Nicu probing around his head in search of the truth.

"Are you afraid?" Nicu asked, the left side of his mouth turned up into a cruel smile.

He considered lying, but knew that somehow, Nicu would know.

"Yes," he said simply. "Yes, I'm afraid."

"And yet you come to me alone to discuss the possibility of release." Nicu leaned back and smiled, breaking the mesmerising spell of observation.

"Curious. Curious indeed."

"Look, I'm no hero. I don't crave the praise of these people. They're strangers I don't even know. All I want is to get home to my family."

"So you come to plead for your own freedom?"

"Yes— No. Look, is there no way we can resolve this situation without people dying?"

"People die all the time, Mr. Garrett. It's the way life is. And how lucky we are that they do, for if not, the world would be a despicable, vastly overpopulated place."

"Look, forgive me if I don't quite follow what's happening here. Frankly, I don't care what you are but—"

"What we *are*, Mr. Garrett?" Nicu said with a questioning smile.

Garrett didn't like that smile. There was something sinister and predatory about it.

"I mean…I don't know," he mumbled, lowering his eyes to the imitation wood of Nicu's desk.

"I think you know well enough what we are, Mr. Garrett, even if those you keep company with do not."

"So tell me. Confirm it," Garrett fired back, risking looking directly into those bottomless eyes.

"Ah, but that would be too easy. I would like to hear it from you."

"Why?"

"Because you fascinate me for reasons I don't yet understand. Now, please, indulge me."

Garrett hesitated, hovering on the fine line between bravery and terror. He looked Nicu in the eye and said the word that had been plaguing him for some time.

"Vampires. I think you and the rest of the people working here are vampires."

It didn't sound as ridiculous as he'd expected now that it was out in the open. In fact, if anything, it made everything feel more real. He waited for a confession, for his slender host across the desk to plead his innocence or admit his guilt. Neither of those things happened. Instead, Nicu sat back in his chair, folded his hands neatly over his chest, and smiled.

LEE / ACCUSATIONS

Donald's recovery was going well. Helen flustered and flapped, the concern in her frightened face doing nothing to ease Donald's guilty conscience which was screaming at him for being such a heartless son of a bitch.

"Helen, for Christ's sake, just relax and stop fussing. I feel fine now."

"You didn't look fine. I thought you were having a heart attack," she said, her voice wavering.

"You won't get rid of me that easy. Please, just relax and go grab a bite to eat or something, okay?"

She wrung her hands nervously, her cheek twitching as she struggled to figure out what to do.

"I'm sorry, I just...I couldn't cope without you, that's all."

The ever present guilt bit him a little harder, and he had to remind himself it was all for the greater good.

"Look, Honey, please. I'm fine. Would you mind grabbing me a coffee?" He pointed to the large self-serve Starbucks machine nestled between the men's and women's restrooms.

"Yes, yes of course. You just wait there. Don't try to move now."

"Honey, please. I'm fine. Do you need any change for the machine?"

"No, no I have some. You just relax and try not to get too overexcited," she said, her face pale.

"I promise, I'll stay right here. Please, I really could go for that coffee right now."

"Of course, I'll be right back," she replied before reluctantly making her way towards the humming vending machine.

As soon as she was gone, Donald turned his attention back to the door to the manager's office which he could just make out from his vantage point at the bottom of the store. Garrett had been gone for a while now, and Donald had made the subtle but definite shift from mild concern to outright worry. Lee walked over and sat on the floor beside Donald.

"He's still not back yet, eh old man?" he said, taking a slow sip of his beer.

"I don't know what you mean."

"Come on," Lee said with a laugh. "The heart attack thing was good but not that good."

Donald struggled to find something else to say, but Lee cut him off with a warm grin.

"Relax, fella. I know why he did it."

Donald decided there was no sense in lying, not after the deceit he had already pulled on his wife, and nodded. "He's been in there for a long time. Maybe too long."

"I wouldn't worry yet. I get the feeling these arseholes need us to keep calm. They can't afford a mass panic."

"So you're saying we should just sit tight?"

"What else can we do, old man? Take a look around, will ya?"

Donald did. Everywhere he looked there were small pockets of frightened people. The only current exception was Bernard, who if anything seemed to be growing more and more confident. He was thankfully out of earshot, but Donald could see by his gestures and the intense way he was speaking that he was either completely unafraid or worryingly crazy. Perhaps he was a little of both. Donald counted seventeen in all that were now listening to him, over half of everyone in the store if you didn't count the broken shells of people walking endlessly around the aisles. Lee continued with a smile.

"These pricks know as things stand they have us under control. We're nothin' to them right now but a bunch of frightened lab rats just waiting for them to finish us off. Course, the other problem is him."

Lee nodded towards Bernard.

"You mark my words now, that wanker might yet cause trouble."

"You don't have to convince me, son. He hasn't shut that mouth of his since you bloodied him up."

"Arsehole deserved it. I'd do it again too."

"I wonder what he could be talking to those people about now."

"I bet I can guess," sneered Lee, before finishing his drink.

"Wrath of god, end of days, beginning of the fuckin' end. Usual shite that comes out of the mouths of people like him."

"People seem to be paying attention."

"Aye. I'm not surprised."

Donald turned towards Lee. "What do you mean by that?"

"Well, fella, he seems to be the only person in here who has a plan. And even though he's the biggest wanker in the building, he could be a problem because, for all his faults, those people are willing to listen to him if they think it might give 'em a chance at getting out of here alive."

"I'm not so convinced. They must surely see he's babbling. Talking nonsense. Hell, I can tell from all the way over here just by the way his lips are moving."

Donald said it more to try to convince himself, as he was afraid to consider Lee might be right. The brawny Irishman only grinned.

"Trust me, fella. When things get down to it— and have no doubts about it, they will— people will want to have somebody they can turn to, and if it's a choice between a man with a plan and the rest of us…well you can guess the rest."

Donald could only muster a nod, and the two sat in sombre silence, stewing over the implications of Bernard leading some kind of fear led uprising. Helen returned and handed Donald his coffee. He sipped from the paper cup and winced, then set it down on the floor.

"Damn, that's hot. Thanks, Honey."

Helen looked mistrustfully at Lee and then back to Donald. "I'm going to see if I can find us some food. Will you be okay for a while on your own?"

"I'll be fine."

"Are you sure? I can stay if you prefer?"

Donald smiled and took his wife's hands in his own and looked her in the eye.

"Helen, please listen to me. I'm fine. I feel fine. I'm okay. What happened before may have just been a flutter, something stress related. You don't need to worry."

"I'm sorry for fussing," she said, just about managing a weak smile.

"It shows you still love me after all these years if nothing else," he replied, giving her hands a gentle, reassuring squeeze.

"Will we be okay, Donald?"

She was searching his eyes, looking for him to say the words she so desperately wanted to hear, but he couldn't face lying to her again.

"I... I don't know," he said with a sigh. "We can only hope."

Her cheek trembled slightly, and she blinked away the tears which he knew from their years together were coming no matter how hard she tried to hold them back.

"I'll go see about that food," she said absently, then pulled her hands free and walked away.

Donald watched her go and realised telling the truth made him feel just as bad as lying to her. He promised himself he would make it up to her if— *when*— they made it to safety. However, that all depended on Garrett and his conversation with the manager. Donald turned his attention back to the door at the end of the market.

"Why did you do that?" Lee asked, taking a battered pack of cigarettes from his pocket.

"Do what?"

"Your old lady." He took out a cigarette and offered the pack to Donald, who waved it away. "Why didn't you just tell her it would be okay?"

"I couldn't face lying to her, not again."

"She didn't know the heart attack was a stunt, did she?" Lee said as he lit the cigarette.

"No. She would never have agreed to it otherwise. Please don't tell her."

Lee inhaled then blew twin plumes of smoke out of his nostrils. "Hey, it's none of my business, fella. I was just curious."

"I'm not a bad husband," Donald said, much more defensively than he intended.

"I never said you were. Truth be known I kinda see your reasons for keeping it from her. Relax, old man, before you give yourself a real dicky ticker."

Lee smiled as he smoked, and although he was still tense, Donald was able to relax a little. They watched as one of the customers— the ones who were mentally broken and walking the store like drones— rounded the corner of the aisle and made her way into the next one. Her eyes were glassy and vacant, and her tongue poked out of her open mouth. It looked shrivelled and dry as she shuffled past on her never-ending shopping trip. Her presence seemed to leave behind a heavy, depressing atmosphere and reminded the two men how dire the situation was. Donald took a careful sip of coffee, and then glanced at Lee.

"So what's your story?" he asked pleasantly.

"No story, fella. Wrong place wrong time just like everyone else."

"I mean why were you here, tonight?"

"What do you mean?"

"Well, we were in here trying the place out as we only live a few blocks away. Ray was doing a few errands for his wife. What about you? What brought you to this store, on this night with the rest of us?"

Lee looked at Donald, and the old man saw there was anger in his eyes and perhaps guilt. There was an aggression in Lee, and remembering he was prying into the private life of a virtual stranger, Donald wished he had never asked. He was about to change the subject to something less intrusive when Lee spoke softly.

"My kid. My kid brought me here."

Donald realised it wasn't anger in Lee's eyes, but hurt.

"What happened?"

"That's a long story, fella. A really, long story."

"Way I see it, time is all we have now."

"I ain't in the habit of talkin' about stuff like this to strangers."

"Maybe it might help? I'm not going to judge you. It seems fate brought us all together for a reason. Maybe the reason was for you to get whatever's troubling you off your chest."

"You're a strange one, ain't ya, old man?" Lee said with a half-smile.

"I just believe in giving everyone a fair crack of the whip. You don't have to talk to me, son. I'm just saying that if you do, I'm willing to listen to you."

Lee smiled, a regretful expression more than one of happiness. "All right," he said as he took another drag on his cigarette. "I'll tell you."

Donald waited. Patient and attentive as Lee organised his thoughts.

"So my kid needs special attention. Around the clock care. Some kind of birth defect or somethin'. Anyways, long and short of it is, she can't walk or do any of the stuff the rest of us take for granted. She…"

He flashed an awkward, pained grin, his throat bobbing as he tried to find the words.

"She…she shits herself. It's not her fault. She can't control it, and she cries when it happens. Really screams the house down… I think that's the worst. When you look her in the eye, you can see she understands and can't do anything about it. Let me tell ya' that cuts me up inside. It just makes me feel so fuckin' helpless. Anyways, things were going okay, right? I mean the three of us, me, my girl, and my kid moved over here from Ireland a few years ago now. We believed all that fresh start, new life shite. But things didn't go as smooth as we hoped, right? But we were getting by. Then last year I lost my job. It was only a shitty bar job, and I hated it, but I did it because I needed to make ends meet. That's what people do, right? They do what they have to. But see, one night my boss was on one of his power trips. He was in my ear all night, just winding me up, trying to get a rise out of me, showing off to his pals about how big and powerful he was, and how much power he had over his staff."

Lee looked at Donald, a haunted smile forming on his lips.

"What it is, fella is that I have a short fuse. Nothin', I'm proud of, but it's just how I am. He kept pushing and pushing. And I tried holding it all together, and even though I wanted to bite his face off, I was doin' okay. I was coping. I was tryin' to think of my girl and my kid, about how important it was to keep my job for their sake. And then he pushed too far. I'll never forget it. He said, *'you are almost as dumb as that retarded kid of yours,'* and that's all it took. I snapped, and I ended up putting him in the hospital for six weeks. I thought that would be it, and I'd be brought up on charges and deported back to Ireland. But the funny thing is he never did anything about it. I don't know if he was scared of what I would do to him, or if he just knew it had been his fault, but for whatever reason, that was the end of it. Or maybe he knew the best way to get back at me was to fire me and watch me suffer. So here I am now without a job. We have rent. Back in Ireland, we had free healthcare. It ain't like that here. We have medical bills to pay for the kid. We have to put food on the table. I tried, fella. I tried to get another job, but my rep worked against me. Nobody would touch me and so…"

He swallowed, and took a last long drag on his cigarette, then dropped it to the floor and stubbed it out under his huge black boot.

"I was left with no choice. They say it doesn't, but when you are on your arse with no other choice, crime pays. I did a bit of this, a bit of that. Anything to scrape enough money to last for another few days."

He turned to Donald, and opened his jacket, revealing a silver handgun strapped into a homemade holster.

"I was here tonight to rob the place, fella. I was here to put some food in my kid's mouth, and if that meant pistol whipping some security guard and frightening a few shoppers, then make no mistake. I was prepared to do it."

He closed his jacket and lowered his head.

"And then all this happened, and here I am— stuck here like everyone else. So go ahead and judge me if you want to, but I didn't do anything I wouldn't do again if it helped to keep my family together."

"It's not for me to judge you, son," Donald said. "You did what you felt you had to, and I can respect that. As for what you just told me, it will go no further, unless you choose to tell it to anyone else."

Lee looked Donald in the eye, his face a mixture of relief and gratitude.

"Thanks, fella. I appreciate it."

He looked as if he were going to elaborate when he saw the door to Nicu's office open. "Looks like our boy is comin' back."

Garrett walked slowly out of the office and began to make his way back towards the main group.

"Your ticker up for a stroll, old fella?" Lee asked with a half-smile.

"Just you try to stop me," Donald said as he got to his feet, arthritic knees screaming in protest.

They met Garrett halfway down the store, and as they approached, Donald could see just how pale and tired he looked. He appeared to have aged impossibly since he first entered Nicu's office.

"How did it go?" Donald asked despite the answer being written all over his face.

Garrett opened his mouth to answer and was silenced by a booming voice from behind.

"There they are!"

The trio turned around to see Bernard pointing at them. Accusing eyes stared from behind him, as a sick grin appeared on Bernard's face.

"I told you! They're scheming against us. Conversing with our captors, whilst we sit here waiting for them to fulfil their false promises."

"Bernard, look—"Garrett began, but Bernard would not be silenced.

"No, you look! First of all, you come to us with these stories of plans and seeking help, and in the next breath you slink away to have private discussions with those who keep us here."

"You need to let me explain—"

"I don't have to do anything," Bernard bellowed, ejecting flecks of spittle onto his chin as he looked at the people, who were again gathered in a rough circle. He seemed to be thriving on the attention.

"You and your group are poison. You're trying to infect us and gain our trust, and then when our backs are turned, you'll hand us over to them," he growled, pointing at the door to Nicu's office.

"Hey, pal," Lee barked. "Unless you want another bloody nose, I'd keep your mouth shut."

Garrett expected Bernard to crumble at this, or at least lose some of his swagger, but instead he seemed to enjoy it. He flashed his twisted smile, a gesture only a whisker away from a horrified grimace.

"Intimidation. More threats of violence. Is this how it's going to be?"

Bernard turned to the surrounding crowd, addressing them calmly, although he was unable to quite drop the too wide, too white grin.

"Are *you* prepared to accept this? Are *you* prepared to let these people decide our collective fate? Because I for one am not."

"Then what *do* you suggest, son?" Donald asked.

Bernard grew serious. The attention seemed to have made him swell, to grow into a giant. He had become a powerful and intimidating presence.

"What do I suggest?" Bernard repeated smugly. "I suggest we stop waiting for those people to come and pick us off one at a time. I suggest we weed out the people who conspire against us and do what's best for the greater good."

He glared at the three of them: Bernard, Lee, and Garrett, and then flashed a wide grin.

"I suggest we offer to them those who would have done the same to us."

Ice filled Garrett's veins. Not only at the cold and emotionless tone in Bernard's voice, but because those watching didn't laugh him off, or claim him crazy. Instead, he felt dozens of pairs of eyes on him and a voice deep inside his mind whispered the words he already knew.

These people are considering it.

"Let me tell you this, fella," Lee said, glaring at Bernard. "You can stand there in that expensive suit and spout as much shite as you like, but let me warn you or anyone else who plans to try anythin' stupid, that I play dirty, and I play to win. You might wanna bear that in mind."

Bernard watched, his smile wavering for a second. Garrett thought that under ordinary circumstances, he would have backed down, but he had an audience now. An audience that seemed interested in what happened next. Garrett had no intention of speaking and didn't realise he was about to until it happened.

"All right, enough!" he said, looking at the ghostly, frightened faces all around him.

"You people have no idea what we are up against. Yeah, it's true I went in there. I won't deny that, but it had nothing to do with some stupid bullshit conspiracy like this crazy son of a bitch is claiming."

A few of the watching crowd seemed less certain and shot each other confused glances. But not Bernard. Still, he stood with that icy grin and unwavering stare.

"I went in there to see if I could negotiate a release, a release for all of us. You were all looking to me, and I didn't know what to do."

"So what happened?" said a leathery, bearded man dressed in khaki combat trousers and a grubby vest. Garrett licked his lips, trying to decide the best way to relay the next chunk of information.

"Look, I didn't want to do this. I know this is going to make me sound crazy and make *him* look like the sanest person in here," he said, nodding towards Bernard, who still hadn't moved.

"This isn't a hostage situation, and these aren't just sadistic murderers."

He hesitated, looking at the people who watched back intently.

"They're vampires."

An incoherent mutter rose, as people spoke in groups. Garrett noticed with dismay nobody had taken him seriously. Some had laughed, others pointed and whispered. Garrett stole a quick glance at Lee, who also seemed to be struggling to hide a smirk. Only Donald remained impassive and watched the proceedings with a concerned frown.

"Why is it such a stretch to believe? Look what's on the damn shelves!" Garrett blurted which even to himself, made him sound like he was a few sandwiches short of a picnic.

"And so, that's our grand revelation!" Bernard boomed, his confident swagger restored.

"We are meant to believe we're held here by the boogeyman."

"Bernard—"

"No, Mr. Garrett. I think we've all heard enough. People are already frightened without you giving us some half-baked tale of monsters and things that go bump in the night."

"You son of a bitch!" Garrett roared and lunged towards Bernard, but Lee grabbed him in a huge bear hug before he could make any real progress.

"Leave it, pal. It's not worth it," Lee whispered to Garrett, who was straining to get to Bernard.

"I'm telling the truth, and that prick is putting everyone's life at risk by laughing it off as a damn joke," Garrett hissed.

Bernard was unwavering. He stood defiantly and watched Garrett with contempt.

"Believe what you will, Mr. Garrett," he said, shaking his head in disdain. "The rest of us— the sane and rational people— will discuss our real options regarding leaving here alive."

Bernard walked away, and Garrett was dismayed to see almost everyone in the store went with him. Garrett stood alone as Lee released his grip.

"You okay, son?" Donald asked.

"Not really, but what else can I do?"

"You can start," Lee said, "by telling us exactly what you found out in that damn office."

Garrett nodded and looked at Donald.

"Are you still with me?"

"I've seen enough in my time to believe anything is possible, son," he said with a warm smile.

"I'd suggest we relocate to a different part of the store, though," he added, nodding to the people who now almost universally glared at them mistrustfully. "I think we've worn out our welcome here."

"Agreed. Come on."

The group gathered by the beer coolers in the alcohol aisle. Garrett looked at the faces of those surrounding him. First the old familiars. Lee, Donald, Helen. There were some new faces, too. They had been joined by the guy in the khaki fatigues who Garrett had spotted earlier and also a young Hispanic man with a poorly maintained caterpillar moustache and a vast landscape of acne scars across his face. They all looked at him attentively, waiting to hear what he knew. He composed his thoughts and began.

"Before I get into it, I need to ask you all to do me one thing."

"Shoot," said Lee around his cigarette.

"He— the manager— told me all about what he is and why we're here. He also said I was free to share the information with whoever I saw fit, something in hindsight was probably a deliberate motion to divide the group which— by the looks of things— has worked. Either way, I'll tell you what he told me. All I ask is you let me finish and get it all out in the open."

"Then what?" asked khaki guy.

"Then," Garrett said, "we get the hell out of here."

"Okay, Ray," Donald said. "The floor is yours."

LEENA

Leena's headache was on the verge of becoming a vicious migraine. It throbbed and probed at the back of her eyes and bored into the centre of her brain. She squinted at the harsh strip lights overhead and wished for darkness, at least until she thought about the people they were trapped with, and then the idea of the dark frightened her. They were too bright, too invasive. She shot a concerned glance towards Mark, but he was no longer speaking and hadn't been for some time. Instead, he stared into oblivion, mouth partially open, the bottle of beer she had given him still held loose and untouched in his hand. She leaned close and looked into his eyes but the smell of his breath— spoiled and pungent— made her recoil. She didn't want to admit it. In fact, *want* was too weak a word. She *refused* to admit he now looked more like one of the others— the broken ones who haunted the rows of produce like slack jawed ghouls. Unable to look at him anymore, she walked the store, desperate to escape from Mark and those blank, sightless eyes. She kept away from the aisles themselves as she knew she wouldn't be able to bear the horrors that lurked amid the otherwise ordinary stock. Instead, she kept to the perimeter, keeping close to the non-edible things. The home furnishings, the CD and DVD section. Things that brought a little normality to an otherwise abnormal world. She had removed her shoes and was enjoying the sensation of cold tiles on her skin when she saw him.

Bo.

He was lurking by the fresh fruit stand. Her heart began to beat ferociously in her chest, and every fibre in her wanted to run, but she willed herself not to show fear. She walked towards him, careful not to break her stride. He watched her come, a frightened girl out of her depth and at the end of her own ability to remain rational and calm. She, in turn, watched him back. A sweating, foul smelling troll who licked his lips and was barely able to hide his excitement as she neared.

She held her nerve and walked past him, keeping her gaze fixed firmly ahead—determined to prove a point. She expected to feel him groping out for her, reaching for her ass or worse, but she remained unhindered and was now safely past him. She exhaled deeply; not realising she had been holding her breath and even allowed herself a smile, a small victory no matter how trivial, was a big deal to her. It was then, with her guard down, that he grabbed her. She tried to scream, but his filthy, fat hand was covering her mouth, and the other was around her waist. She struggled to free herself, but despite his small stature, Bo was incredibly strong. She felt herself being dragged away from the safety of the familiar electronic gizmos— Blu-Rays and iPods and overpriced mobile phones that had apps for everything under the sun— and towards the restrooms. Bo dragged her kicking and struggling into the men's room, the door swinging gently shut behind them.

Nobody in the store had noticed what had happened.

SALLY'S PROMISE

He'd found her slumped in the corner, behind a mound of cheap polyester jackets she'd taken off the rack. At first, he thought she was settling down to sleep, and then noticed the look in her eye.

"How's it going?" Mark said as he sat cross-legged beside her.

Sally didn't answer. Mark's eyes shifted to the bottles in the well she'd made in the blankets between her legs.

"Don't," she said, looking him in the eye. "Just don't say anything."

"You don't need to do this. You have a daughter, we might still get out of this," he said, blinking away tears.

"You don't believe that. I can see it in your eyes. We're all as good as dead."

"But you have to hope. You have to fight."

"I can't. I won't watch those things cut us up. I can't put my little girl through it. Good god, she can't see that."

Sally was crying now, and yet there were no sobs, no sniffles, just a line from each eye. It was almost as if she wasn't even aware she was doing it. He had to fight the urge to reach out and touch them to see if they were real.

"She needs you," he whispered. "You're her mother."

"Remember your promise," she said, eyes wide as she stared at him.

Mark felt his stomach roll. "Wait, just let's see how it plays out, we don't know."

"It's too late. I've already taken them," she said, managing a half smile.

Mark grabbed the bottles, counting three empty ones amid those still unopened.

"You can't do this, you have to be there for her," Mark said, unsure if he was more upset or angry.

"I have to go first. Do you understand?" she said, her words starting to slur. "To meet her. I have to go first."

She lay down. Mark held her hand, transfixed by her pale pink nail varnish.

"I sent her to get another magazine. Told her I was going to take a nap," she said, closing her eyes.

"I can't do it, I thought I could, but I can't," Mark replied, bottom lip trembling.

"You promised. You have to. Don't make me go alone. Send her to me. I'll wait for her. Don't keep her from me."

She drifted off. Mark waited and watched until she stopped breathing. He'd hoped death would bring her peace, yet when he looked at her, he saw her lifeless face screwed into a scowl. Her words echoed back to him, and he knew what he had to do.

Dazed, he'd gone back to Leena, intending to tell her of his promise, to ask her advice. However, he found the words wouldn't come. She gave him a beer, and even tried to talk to him, yet he felt like he was in a bubble, underwater somewhere deep and dark. He was in a place where voices seemed distant and faint, more like whispers from the past. He saw Leena leave, heading barefoot towards the back of the store.

He waited until she was out of sight, then headed to the magazine aisle to fulfil the promise he had made.

II

He used a pillow from the home goods aisle. He tried not to think about what he was doing, even when she kicked and scratched at him. Thankfully he couldn't see it, his vision blurred by tears as he pressed the pillow over her face. When it was done and she stopped kicking, he laid her out under a rack of shirts, putting the pillow under her head and covering her with the blanket.

As he stood, his mind broken at what he had done, he was vaguely aware that nothing that happened to him from then on could be a worse hell than which he'd just experienced. He looked at those who walked the aisles in blissful peace, a zombie-like lack of awareness and thought it might be worth a try. Anything to sooth the absolute shame, guilt and devastation which raced through him. He started to look inwards, seeing how far he could go, looking for something good amongst the darkness he felt inside.

WHAT HAPPENED WITH NICU

Garrett found that his story— as wild and ridiculous as it sounded even to him, was still being reasonably well received by his small party of interested listeners, and so far nobody had walked away, called him a fruitcake, a nut-ball or anything else that would bring his sanity into question. Of course, he hadn't really told them much at all yet, none of the things that mattered anyway, but he knew the time for being selective with his information was over, and no matter how much he was trying to put it off, he had to tell them the part that even he found difficult to believe. He paused and took a long drink of his beer. It was bitter and cold and soothed his throat, which felt dry and sore. He toyed with further delaying telling of the next part, fearing its sheer unreality would either push people over the edge or make him a laughing stock, then almost instantly dismissed the idea. Even so, he wasn't sure how to proceed. Nicu had overloaded him with information, and Garrett was struggling to process it. He half wished he had put off the telling until he had managed to gather his own thoughts. It was too rushed, too soon too—

"Ray."

Garrett blinked, and looked at Donald, who had a concerned frown etched on his tired face.

"Are you okay, son? You seem a little… lost."

It was a good observation. He *felt* lost. His mind swam and pulled in a thousand directions at once. He couldn't concentrate and yet he knew what he needed to say, knew he would be able to articulate it if only he could overcome his own deep-seated fear. He shook his head.

"Sorry, I— I lost my train of thought."

"You were about to tell us about what you said to Nicu when he asked you what you thought he was."

"Yeah." Garrett nodded. "I guess I was."

"Are you okay, son? We can do this later if you don't feel up to it."

"No." Garrett shook his head. "No. It has to be now, or I don't know if I'll ever get it out in the open."

Donald nodded, and not for the first time, Garrett felt the pressure and all eyes were on him, waiting for him to go on.

"Okay. So Nicu asked me what I thought he was…"

"Are you afraid?" Nicu asked, the left side of his mouth turned up into a cruel smile.

He considered lying, but knew that somehow, Nicu would know.

"Yes," he said simply. "Yes, I'm afraid."

"And yet you come to me alone to discuss the possibility of release." Nicu leaned back and smiled, breaking the mesmerising spell of observation. "Curious. Curious indeed."

"Look, I'm no hero. I don't crave the praise of these people. They're strangers that I don't even know. All I want is to get home to my family."

"So you come to plead for your own freedom?"

"Yes— No. Look, is there no way we can resolve this situation without people dying?"

"People die all the time, Mr. Garrett. It's the way life is. And how lucky we are that they do, for if not, the

world would be a despicable, vastly overpopulated place."

"Look, forgive me if I don't quite follow what's happening here. Frankly, I don't care what you are but—"

"What we are, Mr. Garrett?" Nicu said with a questioning smile.

Garrett didn't like that smile. There was something sinister and predatory about it.

"I mean...I don't know," he mumbled, lowering his eyes to the imitation wood of Nicu's desk.

"I think you know well enough what we are, Mr. Garrett, even if those you keep company with do not."

"So tell me. Confirm it," Garrett fired back, risking looking directly into those bottomless eyes.

"Ah, but that would be too easy. I would like to hear it from you."

"Why?"

"Because you fascinate me for reasons I don't yet understand. Now, please, indulge me."

Garrett hesitated, hovering on the fine line between bravery and terror. He looked Nicu in the eye and said the word that had been plaguing him for some time.

"Vampires. I think you and the rest of the people working here are vampires."

It didn't sound as ridiculous as he'd expected now that it was out in the open. In fact, if anything, it made everything feel more real. He waited for a confession, for his slender host across the desk to plead his innocence or admit his guilt. Neither of those things happened. Instead, Nicu sat back in his chair, folded his hands neatly over his chest, and smiled.

"That is quite a leap, my friend," Nicu said, flicking his top lip with a tongue which looked a brilliant shade of red against his pale skin.

"I'm not your friend," Garrett whispered.

"No." Nicu shrugged. "I suppose not."

"So you've heard me say it. Now I want to know if I'm right."

Nicu smiled, and Garrett expected to see razor-sharp teeth, and for his host to launch himself across the desk and attack, but neither happened, and Garrett let his body relax a little.

"Ah, the vampire," Nicu said with a sigh. "The bane of our existence, the curse that has plagued us for centuries."

Garrett felt his stomach drop as if it was filled with stones. He had a bizarre urge to giggle.

"So it's true?"

"Actually no, Mr. Garrett, at least not in the sense that I'm sure your underdeveloped brain has already decided at least."

Garrett said nothing. He was watching Nicu carefully, ready to move at a split seconds notice if he needed to, even if, as he suspected, such a gesture would prove futile after what had happened to the girl who tried to escape. Nicu continued.

"Ever since Bram Stoker penned that troublesome work of fiction, my kind has been plagued with inaccuracies. Indeed, before that even. Idle gossip and folklore, Mr. Garrett, have made the vampire into a romantic, brooding figure, a fictional thing which lives only within the darkness, a noble creature with raw sexuality with which they seduce large chested virgins. Sadly, the reality is very much different."

Garrett found his mind was swimming with the classic vampire references. Bela Lugosi's count Dracula stalking around under cover of darkness in pursuit of Helen Chandler's Mina, or of Vlad the Impaler and tales of his gruesome deeds written in history books, and even more modern versions of the myth. Wesley Snipes as the black half vampire, Blade, and those awful romanticised vamps, where the bloodsuckers sparkle under sunlight and are more interested in love triangles with werewolves than draining blood from their brooding victims. It was enough to make the mind boggle. More so because— according to Nicu— every idea Garrett thought he knew, everything he had prepared for when he came to this office was now redundant. Useless. Worth the grand sum of nothing. He felt sick and looked at Nicu through frightened eyes. Nicu smiled again, the twist of his lips both cruel and somehow elegant at the same time. He wanted to speak but found his brain wouldn't make the connection to his mouth, and so he looked on, waiting for his thoughts to unscramble.

"Mr. Garrett, if it's any consolation you are coping well. Many of your kind breakdown at this point and become gibbering, pleading shells."

"You've done this before?"

Nicu smiled and placed his long-fingered, pale hands on the desk. "Mr. Garrett, try to understand. This is by no means an isolated situation. The people you came here to bargain for, are not special. You are victims of circumstance. All over the world, there are operations much like this one, and almost always there is someone, not unlike yourself who will come forward to try and negotiate for freedom. Many are desperate, pleading beings, ones who quickly become tiresome to listen to. Others try to talk their way out, offering money or possessions, as if we couldn't just take such things if we needed them. And then of course, occasionally there are people like you, Mr Garrett."

"What do you mean?"

"People who come to me with dignity, with self-respect, who listen calmly as they are told what is to become of them."

"We never had a chance, did we?" Garrett asked, unable to keep his voice steady.

Nicu didn't answer. Instead, he smiled.

"What if I kill you?" Garrett heard himself say, unsure where the words were coming from. "What if I kill you right here, right now?"

Nicu snorted, a thin smile spreading across his lips. "You can try, by all means, Mr Garrett. Many before you have, many after you will."

For a split second, Garrett thought about it. He thought about throwing himself over the desk at Nicu, then immediately decided against it. What would he do? He had no weapons, and it was obvious there was little he could do to physically harm Nicu. Worse than all of that was the image of his wife swimming into his mind, the sick feeling of how they parted, and that a stupid argument over nothing could well lead to him never seeing her again, or the birth of his child.

He relaxed, leaning back in the chair. Nicu chuckled as if he had read Garrett's thought process from start to finish.

"Don't be so hard on yourself, Mr. Garrett! You weren't to know escape was impossible and only went by your human instincts. You made the same mistake as those who came before you. You relied on what you know, what culture, television, books, and fiction have told you. You could never have hoped to know the truth. Let me ask you this, if I may. If indeed, garlic was like poison to our kind, would we stock it in our store? If a stake through the heart would be our undoing, would we supply you with the tools to make them? No, no. What we are, what your *perception* of what we are and—more importantly— how to deal with us is, frankly…. laughable."

Nicu pursed his lips and looked at Garrett carefully, and then pointed at him with a long, bony finger.

"I like you, Mr. Garrett. You don't sob and cry and beg like so many before you have. If it puts your mind at ease, I can assure you what I said earlier is true. Even though we could kill everyone in this facility without effort, we will stand by our initial agreement. We do not wish to draw unnecessary attention to our operation. We only need to retain some of you in order to…restock."

"But blood… I mean you need to drink blood to live…" Garrett blurted before he could stop himself. Nicu shook his head slowly.

"Folklore. Stories passed down through your human race, and like the game of Chinese whispers changed so that eventually the truth was lost. However, if you want to know what we are, in terms you can understand, then you can think of our species as a natural evolution of your own. We are stronger, faster, live longer. Impervious to disease. We are without limitations such as remorse. Conscience. We feed on humans not because we have to, but because we choose to. It is our religion. Our way of life. It is not just the drinking of the human blood, but also in the eating of the flesh. The sweet, human meat. That, Mr Garrett, is where we draw our strength. Our vitality. We are able to sustain ourselves on other foods, of course. We can, if required, survive indefinitely without feeding, but Mr. Garrett, who on earth would ever want to do such a thing? Why would we deny ourselves the right to dine on the meat of the inferior? To gorge in the hot bitter blood of those beneath us?"

"So you're… immortal?"

"In terms as you would see it and compared to your lifespan, yes."

"But you said it was all legend. Stories."

"And so it was, or at least back in the dark times. Remember, Mr Garrett, they knew nothing of modern science. Our kind back then was best explained with witchcraft rather than science."

"Science?"

"Of course," Nicu said, seeming a little surprised that Garrett didn't follow. "Evolution, Mr Garrett. Evolution is the key. Our species simply have a much longer lifespan than yours. Whereas you humans may have a life of around seventy or eighty years, the average for my kind is something nearer nine hundred. I will see my two hundred and ninth birthday later this year."

Nine hundred years.

Garrett felt light headed and was certain he was about to faint away, but somehow he regained his composure.

"How did this happen, I mean, where did you come from?"

Nicu smiled. "Nobody really knows, even amongst my people. It seems at some point in mankind's past, something happened which created the first of our species, and all of my kind have grown from there. Sadly, if the first of our kind had the means to chronicle his life, then we are yet to find it. The reason for our being is still shrouded in mystery today as it always has been, and yet, here we are, living in the shadow of a species to which we are its complete superior."

"Why are you telling me all this? What good can it do?" Garrett asked.

"Because I want you to understand. I want you to see that planning to fight, planning to fashion crude weapons with which to attack us is no good, and will result only in unnecessary bloodshed."

"What's to say you won't just kill us anyway?"

Nicu sighed and shook his head. "Mr. Garrett, how many times do you need to be told? You are just a small part of something incomprehensibly large. My kind walk among yours and have infiltrated your human infrastructure from top to bottom. Almost forty percent of the planet is populated by our kind, and you humans are still oblivious. We are your friends, your enemies, your colleagues. Your wives, husbands, and lovers. We are celebrities; we are politicians. We are even world leaders. We walk beside you both by day and by night."

"By day?"

Nicu grinned. "The aversion to sunlight is yet another falsehood, I'm afraid. A convenient addition to the story of our kind to put human minds at ease that their days will be safe. I actually enjoy the warmth of the sun. I own a beautiful home in Florida where I spend a lot of time when I am away from work.

Nicu grinned even wider and lowered his voice to a whisper.

"Believe me, Mr. Garrett. If we so desired it, we could eradicate your species from the face of this planet within a year. But we choose to live in harmony. Unlike you arrogant humans, we don't crave war or bloodshed. We exist, instead, in peace, and— more importantly for your species—in secret. Like it or not, this is the best solution for everyone. Facilities like this one exist in order to supply my kind with their…dietary requirements and to stop the certain bloodbath that would occur if my kind had a free reign to feed as they wished."

"And this facility… what is it? Really?"

"It's exactly what it says on the door, Mr. Garrett. A supermarket. We collect and store our given quota of human flesh which we then sell to our own kind. We never stay in any one place for long. A few months at a time then we close and re open elsewhere."

"But surely someone would notice people going missing?"

"People go missing all the time. Many are never found."

"And that's you? Your people who are responsible?

"Not for all of them, but I would expect many; the ones who disappear unexpectedly without a trace, those are likely down to my kind."

"Who keeps order? Who stops everything falling into chaos?"

"Our kind have our own governments, our own social structures, our own rules, and moralistic guidelines. We make sure any investigations are diverted away from our facilities. Those who get too close are dealt with."

Garrett blinked, unable to process the information.

Nicu chuckled. "Mr. Garrett, did you really think we stalked around in the shadows, drinking blood and snatching people from the streets? No, no. We are a business, an enterprise. And like you humans, we have an economy. A diverse mix of races that have uniquely varied personal tastes. We cater to those races. For over six hundred years, Grueber's has been able to guarantee the freshest, best quality human flesh available. And like it or not, Mr. Garrett, some of you and those you came in here to save *will* be sacrificed for our cause before the doors are opened later tonight. There is nothing that can be done to change it."

"And what if we choose to fight?"

Nicu grew serious, his brow furrowed.

"It's quite simple. If you fight, you die."

"What if you're bluffing?" Garrett said, the tension in the room palpable.

It was then Nicu's face transformed. He grinned. His teeth were still normal; however, he appeared to have another layer of them pushing through the roof of his mouth from behind, and these ones were anything but normal. They were long and sharp. The word shark entered Garrett's head and then wouldn't go away as Nicu's eyes rolled back to the whites. He was a vision of hell. He opened his mouth, and it was impossibly wide. His gullet was a deep shade of crimson as slick strands of drool hung from his chin.

Terror.

Garrett had always assumed he would be quick to react in a life-threatening situation. He had presumed he would be a man of action, the hero of the hour. As he sat there opposite the foul abomination that used to be Nicu, he realised it was all a lie. He was no hero. He couldn't even bring himself to move. In fact, he could do no more than grip the armrests of the chair, as if he were holding on to his very sanity, which in a sense he was because his mind—already privy to so much data, so much incomprehensible horror— was ready to shut down, ready to give up the fight and condemn Garrett to a future of mindlessly wandering the aisles of the market, oblivious to his horrific surroundings and festering in his own shit as he walked around, and around, and around. He could feel it coming, the numb feeling of inability to cope. As he watched Nicu, he felt the scream coming, travelling up from his stomach whilst his exhausted brain was still trying to process what was happening.

Nicu's mouth was still opening, that was an awful enough sight in itself, but now it was also opening sideways. Garrett had heard of snakes with jawbones that were two separate pieces, allowing it to swallow prey much larger than itself, and he thought this must be the same of Nicu and his kind. As Garrett watched, Nicu's jaw was opening outwards, the skin of his chin pulling taut and then stretching and— yes, he could see more teeth at the bottom, twin rows at either side of his normal human ones. There would be no quelling it this time. No quenching for the guttural outburst of terror which was about to project itself, and he dimly thought if he allowed it to escape, then he would surely die. He brought his hand up to his mouth and bit down hard,

hard enough to see white spots dance in front of his eyes. However, it served its purpose, and instead of a scream, he let out an anguished groan. Nicu seemed satisfied, and with agonising leisure reverted back to his more normal self. He looked at Garrett with a teasing half-smile and leaned close. Garrett couldn't help but flinch away.

"I think now you understand the futility of any uprising, Mr. Garrett. Now go. Go and tell your people their fate is decided. Tell them you have until midnight to decide who will be given to us."

II

Garrett looked at the people around him, searching their eyes for any kind of a reaction. He had hoped he would feel better getting it off his chest, but if anything he felt worse.

"And that's it," he said with a sigh. "I came back and did as he asked."

"Fuck!" Lee said, standing and pacing.

Donald looked back to Garrett, and once again, his admiration for the old man grew. He still looked concerned— as would anyone— but he seemed to be coping, perhaps better than anyone else.

"How are you feeling, son?" he asked.

"I really don't know. Okay, I suppose."

"You know we can't do as he asks. We can't just stay here and wait for our turn to die."

"I don't know what other options we have. The place is locked down tight."

Donald nodded and then motioned towards the double doors leading out back.

"What about through there?"

Garrett glanced toward the doors he had fallen through earlier and his mind filled with images of dismembered carcases and severed limbs and the huge, mountain of a butcher busy disjointing Arsenio's troublesome knee.

"I didn't see any exits. All I know is it's some kind of... butchery."

"Staffed?" Donald asked as Lee crouched down to listen in.

"Yeah, the butcher was in there earlier."

"Think we could get past him?"

"I doubt it. The guy was huge. And besides, who knows what it would take to subdue him. I'm not sure we can do it."

"Then we will have to kill him."

The cold tone in Donald's voice shocked Garrett, who was finding his nerves were already frayed to beyond breaking point.

"I doubt sharpened brooms will get us very far. Or didn't you hear what I just told you?"

Garrett instantly regretted saying it, more so the helpless tone in his own voice. Even to himself, he sounded like he had given up. Donald let it slide, and Garrett rubbed his eyes.

"Sorry, Donald, it's just... a lot to take in."

"Forget it, son. This situation is stretching us all to breaking point."

The word *stretching* brought back horrific images of Nicu's gaping maw opening impossibly wide, and Garrett felt his stomach do an involuntary somersault.

"You can say that again," he said simply, hoping nobody had noticed his moment of horrific recollection. "But I suppose escape through the back is as good an idea as any. Tell me what you have in mind."

"Well, I was just thinking about the front door."

"Go on."

"Well it's a low door, right? Narrow. Access wise it's not very efficient."

"I agree, but don't see the relevance."

Donald held his hand up and now he, not Garrett was the centre of attention.

"Look around you, son. The shelves are filled with stock. I'm not talking about the 'other' stock; I'm talking about the stuff all stores hold."

"Yeah. Sorry Donald, but I'm struggling to follow here."

"Deliveries, Ray. Deliveries. No way would they receive them through the front. I'd bet my house on there being a back door we could slip out of."

"All of us?"

"No," Donald replied carefully. "We need to be realistic. Just us." Garrett opened his mouth to respond, but Donald cut him off.

"Now I know it's not ideal, and I know it's not going to be easy to live with if we do make it, but let's be realistic. Those other people have made their choice, and like it or not we have to look after ourselves now and forget about saving everyone."

"And you could live with that?" Garrett whispered.

"Yeah." Donald nodded. "Yeah, I think I could. I'm old, Ray, and I have seen some horrific things over the years. But I'm determined not to die here. Not like this. Not without a fight."

"And you all feel the same?" Garrett asked, looking at the group. Lee nodded. As did Helen. Garrett looked at khaki guy.

"What about you?"

"Yeah. Count me in."

"Okay. You got a name?"

"Cody. Cody Ellison."

"Got it," Garrett said, giving the briefest of nods.

"That just leaves you."

Garrett looked at the Hispanic, acne-faced man with the bad moustache and greasy hair. He shifted uncomfortably and then stood.

"I'm sorry," he said in a heavy Spanish accent. "I have a wife and four children. I... can't risk it."

"You stay here, fella, and you are as good as dead anyway," Lee said, looking the man up and down.

"I can't risk it. At least here I have a chance, what you suggest...is suicide. I'm sorry," he repeated, and then he walked away without looking back.

"And then there were five," Lee muttered under his breath.

Garrett turned back to Donald.

"Okay, so let's assume there is a back door to this place. That still leaves us a huge, butcher-sized problem."

Donald looked towards Lee and tipped him a nod.

"I think our friend here might have that covered."

Lee opened his jacket and showed them the gun. The group let out a simultaneous gasp as if Lee had just performed some kind of incredible magic trick instead of revealing the silver handgun sitting snug against his chest in its holster.

"Okay," said Garrett. "Maybe it's worth a shot. It sure as hell beats sitting here and waiting for them to decide when and how to pick us off."

"Then we should do it soon," Donald said.

"Agreed." Garrett looked at his watch. "It's just after ten now. Let's say half an hour to prepare, and then we make a break for it. Everyone okay with that?"

Heads nodded, and frightened eyes looked on.

"It's important we keep this quiet," Garrett added.

"Why?" asked Cody, wringing his hands nervously.

"Because," Garrett said glancing across the room to Bernard's ever growing group. "There are certain people in here that wouldn't want to see us try for it."

"Maybe we shouldn't wait, and just do it before we have a chance to back out," Helen said weakly, linking hands with Donald.

"I need to do something first," Garrett said, smiling as best he could manage at Helen. "I need to speak to Mark and give him the chance to come with us. It's the least I could do."

"Son, you don't owe him anything. He made his choice," Donald said firmly.

"Regardless of that, some of what he said was right. I need to do what I can. Just give me a few minutes."

Garrett stood and stretched. He couldn't believe how exhausted he felt.

"Lee," he said quietly.

"Yeah?"

"If it comes down to it, if we need you to… are you prepared to use that thing," he said, nodding to Lee's jacket.

"Don't you worry about that, pal. You put any of these fuckin' things in front of me, and I'll drop em' down. That I guarantee."

"Good enough for me."

"Let's just hope the arseholes don't get up again."

Garrett hadn't even considered that as an option and forced himself not to dwell on it for too long.

"We will have to cross that bridge as and when it happens. One step at a time until then."

Lee nodded. "Go do what you need to do, fella, and then let's get outta here. Meantime, I'm gonna go for a piss and grab another beer for the road. Want one?"

"Get me two," Garrett said, clapping Lee on the shoulder. "I shouldn't be long."

MARK

Garrett could smell him before he saw him. He was standing in the corner and staring blankly at the wall. The little girl, Ellie, who had taken a shine to him slept under a clothing rack, blankets pulled up to her chin, face turned to the side. As Garrett moved close to Mark, he noticed he had fouled himself but either didn't care or hadn't noticed.

"Mark," Garrett whispered, leaning as close to him as he dared.

Still, he stared, eyes looking through the wall, mouth hanging open. It was a tremendously sorry sight. The young man with the deliberately messy hair and aviator glasses and that confident, self-assured swagger was gone. In his place was a haggard, broken thing, festering in its own stink and waiting for death to come. Garrett wondered just what it was that had sent him over the edge.

"Mark, it's me. It's Ray."

There was no response. Not even the merest flicker of recognition.

Garrett waved his hand in front of Mark's eyes and clicked his fingers by his ears, but Mark failed to respond. A surprising and overwhelming sadness swept over Garrett, who leaned even closer, doing all that he could to ignore the smell.

"Mark, listen to me. We're getting out of here, or we're gonna try it at least. What do you say?"

He put a hand on Mark's shoulder. "It's not too late. Don't just give up and die like this."

Mark turned his head slowly, first looking at Garrett's hand on his shoulder, and then with what looked to be a monumental effort, looked him in the eye. Garrett somehow kept his expression neutral, but inside, he wanted to scream. Mark's eyes were empty, dull voids. His Adam's apple moved, and he opened and closed his mouth. With an incredible effort to force himself to speak, the words coming in a dry, grating whisper. Garrett leaned close and listened to the cracked words and felt his heart sink as they registered with him.

I deserve to die here. Look after Leena.

"I understand. I'm sorry," Garrett said softly.

He hoped to see understanding or even forgiveness but saw only that blank, vacant stare. He was about to walk away when Mark grabbed onto his arm, his dead man's voice, this time, uttering just four words.

I kept my promise.

Overcome with both guilt and sadness, Garrett found himself choked up at just how confused and disoriented Mark had become.

"I'll look after Leena. I'll do my best to get her out of here, okay? I promise."

Garrett was close to breaking down and realised then that his plan was the right one. Because even though the odds were small, it was better than becoming an empty shell like Mark and the others who had given up or just weren't able to cope anymore.

"I'm sorry. I really am."

"It doesn't hurt this way."

The words cut Garratt deep, and yet made sense. Like some of the others, Mark had chosen to shut himself off, to find a place to await his death and accept it on his own terms. Although they were relative strangers, Garrett couldn't help but feel a bond, one which he'd hoped they would share for a little bit longer. Taking a last look, Garrett turned and headed back towards the others.

NEGOTIATIONS

Lee walked into the oak-paneled restroom, leaned against the sink and let out a deep breath. Away from the prying eyes of the other people who were trapped in their own unique kind of hell, he could drop the act of being a thick-skinned tough guy and acknowledge his fear. He splashed water on his face and looked at his reflection in the mirror. He thought that under the circumstances, he was doing okay, and was certainly holding up better than some. Even though he was doing his best to remain calm, he couldn't ignore the giddy somersaulting sensation of nervous terror which was bubbling in his stomach. He was grateful at least to have the gun. He could feel the comforting weight of it strapped under his jacket, and even though he had only fired it once, he was glad it was there. He had already decided that if it came to it –and their planned escape failed—, then he would turn it on himself.

Suicide wasn't something he had ever considered, and in fact, in the past, he had always had a real problem with those who turned to it as a means of escape. But the last few hours caused him to reassess his opinion because the thought of becoming a slab of shrink-wrapped flesh on sale in this hell hole made the idea of putting a bullet into his brain seem like the easiest decision in the world.

For the first time, he thought he understood a little of why people who without any warning, one day decided to go and find a quiet place to hang themselves, or take a full bottle of prescription pills washed down with booze and drift off into the ever-after. He could even see how those unfortunate victims of the 9/11 terror attacks in New York found it inside themselves to leap to their deaths rather than stay in the burning buildings.

Lee realised when it came to the inevitability of death, it was perhaps better to decide when to bow out on your own terms rather than let somebody else do it for you.

He thought about his daughter, his beautiful baby girl, who might not have all the lights switched on upstairs, but at least he could still look into her eyes and know there was someone in there, someone loving and *aware*, wondering why life dealt such a devastatingly cruel hand. He wondered if he could do it. If he could find it within himself to leave her alone in a world that contained these...*things* that had trapped them. A world so bitter, twisted, and cruel that it thought nothing of taking good people and then chewing them up and spitting them out again.

It was a question he didn't think he would be able to answer until the time came. If his daughter's smiling, drooling face swam out of the darkness of his mind, just as he was about to squeeze the trigger, what would he do then?

He closed his eyes and pushed the thoughts aside. They would do him no good. He splashed more cold water onto his face and was about to leave when he heard a subtle, hollow thud coming from one of the stalls. Lee turned off the tap, plunging the restroom into silence. He turned towards the three white stall doors, which were all closed.

"Anyone in here?" he said, his voice sounding incredibly loud and crisp in the silence of the room. He held his breath and waited, but there was no answer. He took a cautionary step towards the doors, wishing they were the three-quarter length ones with the gap at the bottom so if there was someone— or something— hidden inside, then he would at least be able to see it. He wanted to run, to turn away and pretend whatever he heard was nothing more than a harmless short fuse in his overworked mind, but something inside him—

perhaps pride or even stupidity— wouldn't allow it. Even though his instincts were screaming at him to just go, to get back to the others and leave whoever was in here to their own devices, he found himself taking another cautious step towards the doors and at the same time reaching inside his jacket for the gun. It felt heavy in his hands, and even though he had expected holding it to empower him, it did nothing to settle his nerves. With a trembling hand, he pushed the first door open, holding his breath and waiting for something to leap out and grab him, but the stall was empty. He exhaled and wondered how long his frayed nerves would hold out. He moved cautiously to the next door, straining his ears for any hint of sound. He pushed, but it held firm.

"This one is used, sir," came the quiet, broken English from the other side.

"You okay in there, fella?"

"Yessir, thank you. I just eat too much."

"Sorry, pal."

"No problem, sir."

Lee was about to holster the gun when he saw the T-shirt screwed up in the corner of the room. He recognised the design, white with a silk print of Marilyn Monroe on the front. It was torn across the shoulder, and Lee's instincts bristled to life. Instead of fear, a sudden rage came over him instead, because he knew the T-shirt belonged to Leena. Lee licked his lips and adjusted his grip on the gun.

"Hey, fella, you wanna open the door and let the girl out of there?"

"Go away and mind own business."

"That's fine with me, pal. You just let her out of there, and we can leave it at that."

"Girl mine. Go find own girl."

"I don't think so, fella. You let her out now, or I'm coming in there. You should know I've got a gun, pal, and I'll use it if I have to."

He took a step back, spread his feet and pointed the gun at the door.

"You hear me in there, mate?"

"Yesyesyes. I send out girl!" spat the frustrated, disembodied voice from behind the door.

The lock clicked open, causing Lee to almost pull the trigger, but he somehow held his nerve. Bo had one hand over Leena's mouth; the other was around her bare waist, and he had a short, sharp knife clutched in his podgy grip. Lee tried to assess Leena's wounds as best he could without reacting. Her shoulders and arms were covered in bruises and superficial bite marks, but as far as he could tell none looked particularly deep. To Lee, they bore all the hallmarks of torture rather than to actually cause any real damage. One thing was for sure. Bo wasn't like the others here, at least if what Garrett had said was anything to go by. Lee wondered if he was perhaps some kind of hybrid – half human, half vampire. A slave of sorts destined to live forever to serve his masters. Leena's eyes were wild and frightened, and she stared pleadingly at Lee. Somehow he forced himself to stay cool as Bo pushed her ahead of him, his sweaty, bloated head only just visible over her shoulder.

"See? Girl is okay. You give me gun, and I give you girl," he said from behind his human shield.

"No chance, pal," Lee said, knowing even if he were confident with a gun, the shot would be hard. He couldn't take the chance of hitting Leena. Even so, the way his hands were shaking took the option of firing away from him anyway.

"You give me gun or girl die," Bo barked, glaring over Leena's shoulder.

Lee looked for a shot, any large enough area of flesh he could aim for, however Bo was frustratingly well hidden. Lee had always been good at bluffing. It had got him out of many a tough situation, although the stakes had never been as high as they were now.

"Look, mate, I have my own problems. You leave her be and we'll all walk out of here, and that'll be the end of it. I don't wanna have to kill you."

"You leave now," Bo grunted.

"That ain't happenin', fella. Not without the girl."

"I tell master. Master won't be happy."

"If you don't let her go, you won't see outside o' this room, pal. That I can guarantee. It's your call."

He could hear Bo grunting as he processed the information.

"Okay, okay. You back up. Go to door and I send the girl."

"Fine, fella. Just take it easy."

Lee inched toward the door, keeping his gun and eye trained on Bo, who shuffled after him, holding Leena tight and the blade of his knife pressed against her throat. Lee could see Bo's fat, reflection in the mirrors above the sinks, and saw with dismay he was naked. He didn't want to think too much about what the horrible little man would have done if he hadn't been disturbed.

"Okay, I let girl go now," Bo grunted, releasing his grip on Leena. She sobbed and ran to Lee, hiding behind his arm. He could feel her trembling against him. Lee trained the gun on Bo, who stood defiantly despite his nakedness. He slowly raised his arms with a smug look on his sweaty face.

"I'm going to enjoy eat you. Then I eat her," he said, flashing a sick grin.

Leena was gripping on to Lee's arm, hiding behind him in much the same way as Bo hid behind her.

"Leena, get your shirt," Lee said, nodding towards the corner. Bo started to move the second his eyes were averted, but Lee saw it and turned his full attention back to the piggy little man.

"That's a good way to get yourself shot in the bloody face, fella. You get me?"

Bo glared at Lee but held his ground. Leena retrieved her shirt and pulled it on. She was still trembling and sobbing quietly.

"Now I'm a man of my word. I know you sick, filthy bastards don't understand the idea of respect, but we had an agreement, and I'll stick to it. Now the girl and me are gonna leave. But remember this, fella. If I see your fat, ugly fucking face again, I swear I'll put a bullet between your eyes. Understand?"

"I'll tell," whined Bo, fidgeting from foot to foot.

"I'll tell and they take you first. Then I have the girl!"

Bo was drooling and snarling. Lee didn't think it would come, but he found the ability to unleash a cool, calm smile which he was pleased to see had the desired unsettling effect.

"I look forward to it, you little fuck-ball. Now remember what I said."

"I remember. I remember everything."

Lee and Leena backed out of the restroom and into the relative safety of the store.

II

Now fully dressed; Bo opened the bathroom door, fully intending to slip away quietly and tell his family about the human with the gun. He never had a chance, however, and only registered the flash of the muzzle and the deafening roar of the gun as the bullet sheared away the top of his head. His one remaining eye rolled back as his brains splattered in a claret mist all over the white wall. Lifted off his feet, he slammed the bathroom door which swung open, leaving his twitching corpse lying half in, half out of the restroom. Lee was standing feet spread, shoulders relaxed, and gun poised. He had no issue with what he had done. Granted it had ruined the escape plan, but he knew that he couldn't leave this horrible little man alive, and had to put an end to him.

The roar of the gun had caused a frenzy, and Lee was vaguely aware of terrified voices and the sound of people running. Garrett grabbed Lee by the shoulder and spun him around.

"What the fuck did you do?" he spat, glaring wild eyed at the twitching corpse of Bo.

"I had to, Ray. I had to end him."

The door to Nicu's office burst open and he was there, his face which up until then had been a picture of serene control was now twisted into a mask of rage.

"Kill them all!!" he roared.

"You just killed us, you dumb shit! You ruined everything! " Garrett growled at Lee.

Lee, however, was smiling. Garrett thought he had gone, lost like Mark and the others, but Lee's eyes focused and found Garrett.

"No, I didn't. I just proved they can be killed, fella."

"No good if we're dead too. Come on, let's go. We have to move. NOW."

The two ran to meet the rest of their group. At the opposite side of the store, Nicu and his family started to rampage.

CHAOS

Violence was something Garrett had only really seen in movies or grainy news footage, and as a result, he was completely unprepared for the speed and ferocity with which the fragile peace broke down into chaos. Garrett kept his gaze fixed firmly ahead, and did his best to ignore the screams and the wet tearing sounds which seemed to be coming from everywhere at once. Nicu's staff – his family- who had been up until that point placid, were in frenzy, indiscriminately attacking. Garrett saw the Hispanic man who briefly was a part of their group taken down by two of them, one plunging his teeth into his throat whilst the other held his twitching, thrashing body still. Shelves were knocked over, blood sprayed the goods, ejected at velocity from severed arteries as the rampage went on.

Garrett, Lee, and Leena met up with Donald, Helen, and Cody.

"What the hell happened?" Donald blurted.

"Never mind that now. We have to go!" Garrett snapped, hurrying towards the back of the store. The group made for the black double swing doors that gave onto the concrete preparation area where Garrett had last seen the butcher working on Arsenio's dismembered leg. Garrett was in the lead, Lee just behind with the gun drawn as they tried to distance themselves from the rampage. They were met near the entrance by Bernard, who, like them had set about getting as far away from the bottom of the store as he could. He was wide-eyed and had a perplexed, horrified look about him. For all of his talk and bravado, the single gunshot had dissolved his group, and with it his influence. He now stood alone. Despite the horror of the situation, Garrett felt a smug sense of satisfaction at Bernard's belated epiphany they were in mortal danger.

"I didn't know… how could I know?" He grunted, looking from Garrett to Donald and back again.

"You made your choice, son. Get out of our way," Donald said firmly.

"Let me come with you. Please!"

He sounded desperate, and although Garrett would have loved nothing more than to make him sweat a little, there was no time.

"We can argue about who was right later. Come on."

Bernard nodded and fell in with the group as Garrett barged through the double doors, preparing for his confrontation with the immense mountain that was the butcher. He was relieved to see that the cold, concrete floored room was empty.

"Lee, watch the doors, the rest of you stick close!" Garrett barked, not for the first time wondering how he ended up in command of such a ramshackle group. However, the rest of the group wasn't moving. They were standing in a frightened huddle, trying to process the mind-numbing horror of their surroundings. Garrett had seen it before and was surprised that now on his second visit, he had barely even noticed the array of severed limbs, hollowed out corpses and the stale, copper stench of blood.

In an ideal world, he would have warned them in advance, told them to prepare themselves for what lay ahead. However, that was before, in a lifetime before Lee changed things by shooting Bo in the face. Even Bernard now looked as broken and frightened as the rest of them as he tried to understand the true horror of his surroundings. It was as if someone had let the air out of him slowly, and he was now a deflated shell of a man who, like the others couldn't take his eyes from the grizzly display that surrounded them.

"Donald, come on!" Garrett croaked, his eyes flicking to the double doors and knowing there was little time before Nicu's staff were onto them. Donald blinked, and then he was moving, grabbing Helen by the arm.

"Where? I don't see a way out." He grunted.

There was a door behind the countertop where Garrett had last seen the butcher and a corrugated steel door to the loading bay which looked to be run electronically. On the floor in front of the door was a dried trail of blood. It was plain something had been dragged through at some point in the recent past.

"See if you can open that loading bay door. Lee, you come with me and see what's in there," Garrett said, pointing to the closed door behind the counter.

"Bernard..." he began, but Bernard wasn't listening. He was still staring at the dismembered limbs, his mouth moving, perhaps in silent prayer to whatever god he believed in. Garrett could see his mind trying to process the signals sent by his eyes and rejecting them. He supposed it was hard for Bernard. For a man who seemed to live by the rules of rationality and order, he was having a particularly tough time of making sense of being trapped in a nest of flesh-eating vampires who were now pissed off and coming for them.

"Bernard!" Garrett repeated, actually feeling a little sorry for the man. "Dammit!"

He shook his head, knowing any attempt to communicate was, for now, a lost cause.

"Cody, you watch the door and keep your eyes peeled for anyone coming this way."

Nobody argued. They were too afraid to think for themselves, and so did as they were told. Donald, Leena, and Helen made for the loading bay door. Bernard continued to stare and try to make sense of his surroundings. Garrett hurried around the bloodstained countertop, Lee with him. He grabbed the door handle, and then looked Lee in the eye.

"You ready?"

"Yeah."

Garrett swung the door open, and the pair stepped inside. The room was a small and unremarkable office, containing a single table at the far wall and a bank of monitors offering views of the store from various security cameras. A second door was halfway open and revealed the top of a descending staircase.

"Lee..." Garrett said, nodding towards the staircase.

"Got it," Lee replied, moving to the open door with the gun held out in front of him. He ducked his head through the doorway.

"Fuckin' stinks of shite down there."

Garrett agreed. He wrinkled his nose at the somehow sweet, yet bitter smell and somehow managed to swallow the urge to vomit. The walls of the staircase were bare stone and wet with damp. Garrett couldn't shake the uneasy feeling surging through him as he looked down to the faint light from below where the steps curled away out of sight, that something down there was looking back.

"Well fella, whaddya think?"

"No, not yet. Let's see if Donald can get the door open before we go down there."

"No arguments here, pal. You think there's anyone down there?"

"I hope not."

"What about this butcher fella?"

In all the confusion and blind panic, Garrett somehow forgot about him already. Perhaps he was subconsciously blotting the one real obstacle to their chances of escape out of his mind.

"He could be down there. I haven't seen him anywhere in the store."

"But we can't be sure?"

"No."

Lee lowered the gun and turned to Garrett.

"You want me to poke my head down there and check it out?"

Garrett paused, and then shook his head.

"No. Not if we don't need to."

Garrett turned to head back to the others when Lee put a hand on his shoulder.

"Look, pal, between you and me, I'd rather not take the others down there unless we know what we're dealing with."

"I hear ya. And for the record, I'd rather not go down there at all, unless we have to. Believe me, it's an absolute last resort. Let's see if we can get the loading bay door open first, okay?"

"Whatever you say, fella. You go on. I'll wait here and make sure our butcher friend doesn't sneak up on our arses."

"Keep your eyes open."

"You don't need to tell me twice, mate. Go on now. See to the others."

"The controls are operated by key," Donald grunted between gritted teeth. "Gimmie a hand!"

Garrett hurried over, hooked his fingers under the metal sliding door and gave his all, but even with their combined strength, they couldn't move it. It was securely locked in place.

"Forget this. It's not working, back to the store!" Garrett blurted.

"No," Cody said, turning back to the group. He turned away from the window. Garrett could see from his ashen face that something was seriously wrong.

"We can't go back. Not in there."

Garrett started towards the door to see for himself.

"Don't. You don't need to see what's out there."

Garrett nodded and turned back towards the group. They were now watching him and waiting to be told what to do.

"We're trapped here, aren't we?" Donald asked.

"Not quite. There's a staircase in the back. It could lead to a way out."

"Please," Leena said, looking from Donald to Garrett with frightened eyes. "Please don't let them get me."

She was shaking, and her eyes had a glassy sheen.

She's close to the edge, Garrett thought to himself, and then realised the same could be said for all of them.

"We should try for it."

Everyone looked at Bernard, who had regained enough of his composure to find his voice. He looked at the group, who were now staring at him and even found it in himself to give the smallest flicker of an arrogant smile.

"I mean, what other choices are there? It's either take our chances down there or wait here to be killed. And I for one have a hell of a lot I want to live for."

Nobody said anything, and for a few seconds, they stood and listened to the screams and brittle tearing sounds from the adjoining room. Donald took his wife by the hand and stepped forward.

"We should get moving. We don't have time to stand around here and think about it."

"I don't think I can do it," Leena said simply.

She somehow managed a pained, haunted smile. "I really don't think I can. I'm sorry."

Helen reached out and took her hand. "Come on honey, we can do this together. You just keep a hold of my hand, and everything will be all right."

The older woman smiled as calmly as she could manage, and although Leena didn't say anything, she nodded her head.

"Okay. Let's go," Garrett said, hurrying to the door.

Lee was still standing with his back to the edge of the doorframe, peering down the steps.

"I take it the loading bay is out?"

Garrett nodded. "It's not happening. Any movement down there?"

"Not a thing, just that bloody awful smell. How do you want to do this?"

"What do you mean?"

"I mean, do we go slow and quiet, or run for it?"

"If we can get out of here and keep under the radar, then I'm happy with that," Garrett said. "Besides, I'm sure Nicu and his family will be out there looking for us. You in particular, after what happened with Bo. I don't think it will take too long for them to realise we have slipped away."

"Aye. Best get moving then."

Lee went first, followed by Bernard then the three-person chain of Donald, Leena, and Helen, who were all holding hands. Cody came next with Garrett at the rear. The staircase was narrow, and the slick walls were black with damp. Nobody spoke. Instead, the group concentrated on descending and straining their ears for the slightest noise that might alert them to any potential surprises.

After what felt like an eternity, they reached the sub-basement, which was a rectangular concrete room filled with stacked crates of canned goods and packages of coffee and pasta. The wall furthest from them was dominated by two large silver fronted walk in freezers. To the right, the room extended and there was another door that looked to lead to a small single windowed office. All of this was inconsequential, however, as their attention was drawn to the huge hole in the floor. The concrete had been broken up and removed, and from the bare earth below a roughly hewn staircase was visible. Frightened eyes looked at each other and then came to rest on Garrett. He peered down into the opaque emptiness and wrinkled his nose at the horrific, rotten stench that drifted from there.

"I can't do it. Not down there, no way." Leena was shaking and stared pleadingly at Garrett. Helen squeezed her hand and tried her best to comfort her, but she too was afraid.

"Lee, check that office door," Garrett said softly. "Cody, open those fridges. See if there's anything in there we can use as a weapon.

Both men went to their respective tasks without question. Lee rattled the door handle to the office.

"Locked," he said, as he peered through the small window. "No way out that way."

Garrett turned towards Cody, who was standing at the open freezer door. Garrett and Donald saw his expression and shared a troubled look.

"Wait here," Garrett said to the group, crossing the room to stand beside Cody, who was staring into the freezer.

There were *things* in there. Things that used to be people, humans like everyone else. Now they were just meat. Row upon row of carcases hanging from huge, stainless steel hooks. Many were only partial remains and Garrett again felt the hysterical urge to laugh bubbling up inside him. He cast his eyes over the… Stock? Goods? Remains? He couldn't find the word. Perhaps, there wasn't one that would do justice to the things he could see.

An arm.

A leg.

A skinned, half ribcage.

A limbless torso.

Those things were bad enough, but nowhere near as awful to see as the bodies that were complete. Disembowelled and hanging, eyes open and covered in a light dusting of ice, mouths gaping in a frozen, never ending scream. Garrett had a bizarre idea he was looking into the future, the future of his group. He felt his stomach roll, jump and roll again and knew he was going to let out that giggle—or perhaps it *was* a scream after all— that rolled around in there. He knew how it would sound. It would be shrill and intense and he knew its arrival would see the end of any rational thought or sanity left within him. He had seen enough— more than enough— but he couldn't tear his gaze away. Even if he could it wouldn't matter. Because the image of those dismembered, swaying corpses was one that would stay with him for the rest of his life, no matter how long or short it would go on to be.

"Cody," whispered Garrett.

Cody didn't respond. He simply stared, doing the best he could to cope, process and hang on to his sanity.

"CODY," Garrett repeated more firmly. He looked at Garrett, and for a moment, they were mirror reflections, each sharing in the other's horror.

"Close the door. Come on," Garrett said as he lay a reassuring, shaking hand on Cody's shoulder.

"What is it, what's in there, fella?" asked Lee from the other side of the room.

Garrett shook his head, unable to find any words that would even begin to explain.

"Son, what is it?" Donald said, starting towards them.

"No," Garrett said, perhaps a little too sharply. He softly closed the freezer door. "Nobody should have to see that."

Silence.

Garrett looked at the group and wondered if any of them really knew how grave their situation was. He supposed it might be a blessing of sorts that they didn't.

"Okay then," Bernard said, clapping his hands together. "We either go down, or we go back. Fifty-fifty choice people."

Garrett noted how— much to his disdain— Bernard seemed to have a much better grip on himself now, and if anything actually seemed to be the most composed of them all.

"We can't go back. That's not an option," Garrett heard himself say from some distant place.

"Okay then. Down it is," Bernard shot back sharply, Keeping eye contact with Garrett and even flicking that arrogant smile in his direction.

"I CAN'T!" Leena wailed, breaking into huge, shaking sobs. Helen held her close and stroked her hair, then looked to Garrett with eyes that were just as afraid.

"I agree. I'm not prepared to go down there. Nothing good can come of it." She shook her head and looked at Donald, who nodded in agreement.

"Well somebody needs to go down there and see if it's safe!" snapped Bernard, his lip twitching as he glared at the group.

"Don't let us stop you, arsehole," Lee muttered.

"What about you, big man? Bernard shot back. You're the one with the weapon after all."

Bernard's tone was mocking, and he looked at Lee with a sly, oozing smile. "What's the matter? Not so brave now, are you? Pathetic."

Lee stepped towards Bernard, who took a compensatory step back and snorted down his nose.

"What? Are you going to resort to violence again? Is that the only response you have?"

"Don't push me, you prick!"

"Oh, please." Bernard sneered, shaking his head. "You're brave enough waving that weapon around but how much courage do you have when it really matters?"

"That's enough!" Garrett snapped. Bernard paid him no attention. He was glaring at Lee with a secretive, snake-like smile.

"You don't understand. I have a daughter…" Lee mumbled.

"Oh, and I can only imagine how *proud* she is of her gutless excuse for a father."

Before Garrett could intervene, Lee was pointing the gun at Bernard's head.

"Tell you what, fella," Lee said, flashing a nervous half smile. "Why don't you do the honours for the rest of us and go down there and take a look?"

Bernard held his hands up, but he was still smiling and made no effort to move.

"Lee, take it easy," Garrett warned, unable to keep his eyes off Bernard, who looked completely unconcerned.

"Stay out of this, fella. This is between him and me."

"Is it?" Bernard asked playfully, tilting his head to one side. "Is it really about the two of us or is it about you, and the fact that despite the tattoos and the cliché biker getup, you're a failure, a waster. A god-damn loser, drifter just like every other drain on society, on hard working people like me."

"You shut your mouth!" Lee roared, aiming the gun with much more intent at Bernard's face.

"Lee, please..."

"Don't worry, Mr. Garrett," Bernard smiled. "He doesn't have the fortitude to pull the trigger. I'd bet my life on it."

"I'm warning you!" Lee said, his hand shaking as he aimed the weapon. Bernard only smiled and shrugged his shoulders.

"Warn as much as you like." He sighed. "We both know you won't pull the trigger."

"Lee, just relax and put the gun down, please," Garrett said softly, trying to diffuse the situation.

"This prick is asking for it! He's been asking for it all fuckin' night!"

Lee glared at Bernard, who watched on in quiet amusement, seemingly oblivious to the tiny thread by which his life was hanging.

"Lee, come on. Give me the gun. Think of your daughter."

Garrett was sure his words went unheard, and regardless of them, Lee was going to do it. Garrett held his breath, expecting at any time he would see Bernard's smug face explode in a mist of blood and bone.

"Yes. Think about your daughter. Do as your fearless leader tells you," Bernard taunted, stepping forwards and pressing his forehead to the barrel of the gun.

Garrett and the others looked on in disbelief. It was obvious by now Bernard was crazy. He must be, because even though Lee was just a half-pound of pressure away from ending his life, Bernard had somehow managed a wide, Cheshire cat grin.

"We can't stand here all day," Bernard taunted. "Either do it or don't. Just make the decision so we can move on."

Lee gritted his teeth and glared at Bernard.

"Fuck you."

Garrett knew Bernard had pushed things too far and was about to pay for it with his life. Lee pressed the gun harder into Bernard's forehead and held his breath, then exhaled deeply and lowered the gun.

"Sonofabitch" he grunted, handing the gun to Garrett.

Everyone visibly relaxed, and whatever spell there was, had been broken.

That was a close one.

The thought had entered Garrett's mind as he turned towards Donald to hand him the gun for safekeeping when there was an almighty roar of gunfire. Garrett spun back around, at first sure the weapon had somehow gone off in his hand. As he began to understand what had happened, it played out in a series of snapshots in his brain.

Bernard standing, feet apart, arms straight, in the trained pose of a man who is both familiar and comfortable with shooting weapons.

The black pistol that had been holstered in his jacket held confidently in his hands, a thin wisp of smoke coming from the barrel.

Lee's eyes rolling back into what remained of his skull, the entry hole visible just above the right eye; the bullet's exit painted in sharp ruby red on the wall behind him.

Leena's piercing scream, and then the smell.
The smell of sulphur. The smell of smoke and burning blood.

Then there was Bernard. His face twisted into a horrific, twitching cheeked rictus of defiance, the grin of a man who has lost his sanity, a man who is desperate enough to do anything to save his own skin.

The entire scene lasted only seconds. They watched as Lee fell to the ground, the little that remained of the back of his skull hitting the concrete with a thick wet slapping sound that brought the recently averted nausea flooding back. The rest of the group looked on in silence, unsure how to react to the unexpected turn of events. They looked from Lee to Bernard. Lee to

Bernard again. Still trying to process, still trying to understand.

Garrett would have bet his life there would be screams, mass panic, and chaos. Instead, everyone stayed where they were. Everyone looked at Bernard with open-mouthed surprise as if he had just performed some incredible magic trick, or given some profound statement that required a moment to just stand back and consider. In a way he had, because in the space of a few short hours, Bernard had gone from irritating, stubborn stranger, to frightened survivor, to murderer. Bernard was still smiling as he looked at Garrett.

"Hand over the weapon please, Mr. Garrett," he said calmly.

Garrett looked at the gun held loosely by the barrel in his hand. He was still trying to come to terms with what he had seen when he was suddenly eye to eye with Bernard's own gun.

"You were armed... all this time, you were armed…" Garrett muttered.

"Don't make me ask you again, please."

Garrett glanced at the shocked and frightened faces of the group, then at Lee, a small curl of blue smoke seeping up out of the entry wound above his eye. Then at Bernard. Bernard who was wild-eyed and desperate and who would have no issue with putting a matching hole in Garrett or indeed any one of them. Seeing no other choice, he numbly held out the weapon to Bernard, who took it and expertly ejected the magazine, kicked it across the floor then tucked the unloaded gun into the waistband of his pants.

"Thank you," Bernard said softly. He then motioned towards the bare earth staircase in the floor and smiled at Garrett. "Now, go down there and find a way out of here, please."

Garrett moved cautiously to the top of the steps, trying his best to ignore both the pungent odour from below and the unseeing eye of Bernard's gun, которая was trained on him.

This wasn't how it was supposed to be, he thought to himself as he looked at Bernard, hoping to see even a shred of humanity that he could appeal to, but his eyes were blank and Garrett knew reason was no longer an option.

"Look, you don't have to do this. We're not the enemy. We need to stick together. If we—"

"No, Mr. Garrett, no more talking. We've wasted enough time listening to you already. Now we're going to do things my way."

"Bernard, please…"

"Go NOW, Mr. Garrett. I won't ask you again."

"Why are you doing this? We're on the same fucking side!" Garrett spat.

"Don't preach to me!" Bernard snarled. "If I hadn't found you upstairs, then you would have left me to be killed by those… those things."

Bernard pointed at Garrett, and tiny flecks of spittle shot out of his mouth as he spoke.

"Well, let me tell you something. Bernard Winthorpe does *not* lose. Especially to the likes of you. Now are you going to do as I ask or do I have to shoot somebody else?"

"No. No, I'll go. Just…relax, okay?"

Garrett crossed to the first uneven dirt step and peered into the darkness. It was inky and pure. The bare earth walls were moist and somewhere below him; he could hear a steady, repetitive dripping. He took another tentative step and cast a quick glance over his shoulder at the rest of the group. He forced himself not to look at Lee's body, and then he turned back to the task ahead and took another step down.

"Oh, Mr. Garrett," Bernard said with a wicked smile. "If you do find a way out, and have any ideas about taking the selfish route…"

He held the gun so Garrett could see it, and then rolled his eyes in the direction of the group.

"Message received, you son of a bitch."

"Good. Now go."

He stood there frozen, unsure if he would be able to will his body to move him down into the darkness below, but something in him told him that Bernard would have no hesitation in killing again, and he was likely the next target. With that in mind, he took a last look around the room and descended into the darkness.

ENDGAME

The wait for Garrett's return felt painfully slow, but in reality, was less than ten minutes. They heard him first, his rough breathing heralding his arrival. He scrambled back up the steps, dirty and exhausted, screwing his eyes closed against the light.

"I think I found a way out." He panted.

"What's it like down there, son?" Donald asked, subconsciously pulling Helen close.

"It's like nothing I can describe," Garrett said, shaking his head.

"Did you see anyone else down there?"

It was Bernard. He was crouched by the hole, his eyes burning into Garrett's brain. He forced himself to meet Bernard's gaze.

"I didn't see anyone, and I sure as hell didn't go calling out to see if anyone answered. Just hurry up and keep quiet, and we can get the hell out of here."

Bernard seemed convinced and nodded slowly, a half-smile still etched onto his lips.

"Then let's go. But remember this. If you're deceiving me… I'll put a bullet in you. And that's a promise."

"I get it, Bernard," Garrett said with a dejected sigh. "You win. I lose. I don't care. I just want to get the hell out of here and back to my normal life. Now are you coming or not?"

He didn't wait for a reply. He simply turned and trudged back down the steps and stopped at the bottom. The rest of the group followed, eying Bernard cautiously as they passed. He watched them go by, keeping the gun trained on them as he joined the back of the line.

The bottom of the steps led to a long, uneven corridor carved out of the dirt which descended on a gentle downhill gradient. It was too short to stand upright in, and the group shuffled along hunched over and in silence, feeling their way across the rough walls. Garrett led them down, trying to ignore the increasingly foul stench as they went deeper.

"Be careful. More steps here."

Garrett's whispered voice drifted to them as they moved further into the darkness. The second set of steps were even narrower and steeper than the first as they went deeper than the foundation of the supermarket. Now they could see thick, gnarled tree roots curving in and out of the walls, and could feel the pressure of the weight of the building above their heads.

Still, they descended— a terrified conga line holding on to each other in the darkness. Even Bernard had withdrawn slightly, some of his inherent crazy replaced by fear as the group inched deeper.

"I thought you said there was a way out. We seem to be going straight down," Cody croaked, his voice high-pitched and frightened.

"Keep it down, damn you," Bernard hissed.

Still, they went on, feeling their way through the claustrophobic tunnel and the ever increasing foul stench. The darkness eventually began to give way to a dull orange glow, the flicker of light subtle at first then slowly growing in intensity as they neared, so that at last they could see where they were walking.

"Okay," said Garrett breathlessly as he came to a halt and turned to face them. "Try not to look too closely at anything in here, okay? For your own good."

Nobody answered, and he took their silence for agreement. He led them on.

The tunnel opened up into a huge round antechamber which had been carved out of the earth. Around its perimeter hundreds of candles flickered and danced, casting grotesque shadows across the uneven walls. The chamber floor was covered in human remains. Many were only bones, picked clean and stark white. Others still had skin and were brown and leathery; the half-eaten cadavers partially mummified. Worse than all of those were the fresh bodies. Although perhaps fresh wasn't the right word, for they were putrid with decay, bloated and ruptured and covered with maggots, which combined with the shadows cast by the flames of the candles, seemed to give them a new, undulating life. The steady drone of flies made a suitable auditory backdrop to the scene, which was only slightly less disgusting than the rancid ammonia smell, which was almost unbearable.

In what appeared to be a grisly form of decoration, fully formed human skins were stretched around the room, tied to each other at the arms and feet in some kind of primitive wall covering.

"Sweet Jesus in heaven," Bernard muttered, the gun forgotten and hanging limply at his side.

"This must be where they feed," Garrett said quietly, picking his way through the tangle of corpses that covered the floor. "Come on. It's this way."

They followed in silence. Across the room was another narrow tunnel, which was cut from the earth. Garrett paused by the entrance and waited for the group to pick their way through the corpse littered ground and join him. There was a heavy silence broken only by the soft sound of Leena's weeping.

"This is our way out," he said, looking at their haunted faces as they gathered around. Bernard strode over, poking his head into the tunnel and glaring at Garrett.

"This one goes even deeper. I told you not to screw with me," he raged, pointing the gun at Garrett's head.

"Relax. Hold your hand out."

Bernard eyed him mistrustfully, and then did as Garrett asked, holding his non-gun arm over the tunnel entrance.

"Do you feel it?"

"Yes," Bernard replied, his small smile growing into a relieved grin. "Yes, I do. A god-damn breeze!"

"Exactly. Our way out."

"Perhaps," Bernard said, his smile melting away. "You first. Go down there and make sure."

"Are you crazy?" snarled Garrett. I did everything you asked. I'm done."

Bernard took a step forward and shoved the barrel in Garrett's face.

"You're done when I say you're done. Now go."

"No. If you want to get out, then you take the lead. I'm through."

"I'm in charge here," Bernard snapped, his words reverberating off the walls.

"Actually, *I'm* the administrator of this facility."

As a group they turned to see Nicu standing by the steps, arms folded in front of him. His face was covered in blood from the frenzy in the market.

Bernard let out a high-pitched whine, which built into a horrified scream, and fired off five consecutive shots at Nicu, emptying the weapon, but this time it wasn't with the same cold assurance with which he had killed Lee, but the wildfire of a frightened and cornered man, and as a result every shot missed its target. Nicu didn't even move. Bernard carried on trying to fire even though the gun was empty, and as his scream petered out, and he realised what had happened, he lowered the weapon, breathing heavily and staring at Nicu.

"This could all have been avoided," Nicu said pleasantly as if the incident with Bernard hadn't even happened.

"All of the bloodshed. All of the...petty violence. It's all so...Neanderthal."

He walked towards them, the tangle of corpses at his feet doing nothing to slow his graceful approach.

"We have to run. We have to go now!" Donald said, grabbing Leena by the arm. Nobody moved. Everyone was rooted to the spot, perhaps in fear, or hopelessness or the sheer magnetism which poured from Nicu as he watched them with calm assurance. He seemed more at home here, more comfortable in this chamber surrounded by the remains of the dead than upstairs in the supermarket.

He smiled as he walked among them hands clasped behind his back, and Garrett was again astounded at how regal he appeared.

"In a way, it's such a shame. Mr. Garrett did almost lead you to the way out. That passage, so close yet so far, does indeed lead to the freedom you so crave.

Sadly, it is a freedom you will not taste. Not all of you at least."

The butcher, huge and barrel chested, lumbered out of the tunnel, almost completely filling it as he stood at the entrance with his arms folded. The group watched with dismay as the rest of Nicu's staff walked down the steps from the supermarket, their footfalls making no sound whatsoever as they joined him in the circular chamber. Nicu walked toward the group, looking at each of them in turn. He paused in front of Garrett.

"You brought them so close, Mr. Garrett, so very close to their freedom."

Nicu stood back and looked at the rest of the group, and that horrible, knowing smile reappeared.

"Do they know their deaths have paid for your freedom?"

All eyes fell on Garrett, who in turn lowered his gaze. Nicu grinned and clapped his hands together.

"Ahh, the sweet moment of realisation. Tell them, Mr. Garrett, of our arrangement."

Garrett couldn't face them. Instead, he remained silent and tried to ignore the bitter taste of guilt which was almost as sour as the hostile and disbelieving stares of the group. Nicu was enjoying the moment, grinning as he walked leisurely among them.

"Since Mr. Garrett seems reluctant to divulge exactly what I refer to, then perhaps you will allow me to explain on his behalf."

"Don't… please…" Garrett said, still gazing at the floor and wishing it would open up and swallow him. Nicu smiled and continued.

"When Mr. Garrett came to see me earlier, we had a discussion, as you know, about your freedom. However, what he neglected to inform you is there was more to our discussion than he chose to divulge…"

There would be no quelling it this time. No quenching for the guttural outburst of terror which was about to project itself, and he dimly thought if he allowed it to escape, then he would surely die. He brought his hand up to his mouth and bit down hard, hard enough to see white spots dance in front of his eyes. However, it served its purpose, and instead of a scream, he let out an anguished groan. Nicu seemed satisfied, and with agonising leisure reverted back to his more normal self. He looked at Garrett with a teasing half-smile and leaned close. Garrett couldn't help but flinch away.

"I think now you understand the futility of any uprising, Mr. Garrett. Now go. Go and tell your people their fate is decided. Tell them you have until midnight to decide who will be given to us.

"What if I want to make a deal? For my own freedom," Garrett asked, forcing himself to lock eyes with Nicu, who in turn clapped his hands together and threw his head back in laughter.

"Wonderful! What do you propose?"

"I have a group with me," Garrett said, knowing he had no choice now but to bargain for himself. "Small right now, but they're looking to me as a leader. They trust me. If you give me some time, I can get more, maybe five or six in all."

"And all you wish for in exchange is your own freedom?"

Garrett nodded, feeling his gut tighten as he went on.

"I have a family. If it means stepping on a few people I barely know, then I'm fine with that. I'll do whatever it takes to get back to my wife. As I said, they trust me. I can use that."

"Very good, Mr. Garrett! Very good indeed!" Nicu said, obviously enjoying the unexpected turn of events.

"Look, I'm not thrilled about it, but I'll do what I have to if it means I get out of here. How do you want me to do it?"

Nicu thought for a moment, pressing his index fingers together and tapping them against his lips.

"The most obvious way is a staged escape, I would think. Perhaps through our butchery preparation area? Guide as many as you can into the catacombs below the supermarket. Take them to the room below the sub-basement and you shall have your freedom. You shall not be harmed, nor stopped or obstructed by any of my staff, although it would be in your interests to behave appropriately in order to 'sell' the illusion. Are we in agreement?"

Nicu held out a wiry, long-fingered hand, which Garrett shook cautiously. He expected it to be cold, but Nicu's skin was surprisingly warm – another vampire myth dispelled.

"I'll do it," Garrett grunted. "I'd ask for a guarantee, but I suppose I have to take you on your word here."

"Yes. I'm afraid you will need to show a little faith, Mr. Garrett. Just like the faith your friends showed you," Nicu replied, enjoying the way Garrett squirmed as he said it.

"I still don't understand. What's in it for you when you can obviously just kill us all anyway whenever you choose?"

Nicu shrugged.

"We are not a greedy race. We take only what we need to. Besides, in our experience, flesh that has tasted even the faintest glimmer of hope is all the sweeter. It gives a certain...delicate flavour."

"But that still doesn't explain why you have agreed to let me live."

"Isn't it obvious, Mr Garrett?"

"No."

"It's quite simple. I believe this world is a much better place with people such as yourself in it. A man who will give away the lives of people who trust him without a thought for their well-being in order to save himself is both rare and...refreshing."

Nicu grinned, but Garrett remained stony faced.

"I don't care about any of that. Just get me out of here alive, and I'll deliver you the people. Just make sure your staff knows not to tear us to pieces before I can get them to the sub-basement. I'm sure you appreciate convincing them won't be easy."

Nicu began to laugh. "And they call us monsters!"

Garrett didn't reply. He remained stony faced as he fought with the moral consequences of his decision.

"Very well, Mr. Garrett. We are in agreement. Go now and do as you will. Get the rest of your group to the catacombs. Give them their hope and you will earn your freedom.

"What about the door in the butchery. The metal one for deliveries. I saw it earlier. They'll want to try for that. I need to be able to convince them to go to the sub-basement with me."

"Don't worry about the door. It will be secured."

"And the butcher?"

"He won't trouble you, although it may be beneficial for you to keep the threat of him close to ensure they follow your lead."

"All right," Garrett said, standing on legs which felt like they would collapse under him. "Then we have an agreement. Give me some time to convince them."

"Very good, Mr Garrett. I look forward to watching this scenario unfold."

Betrayal.

The guilt hurt Garrett a lot more than he could ever have imagined. All along he had convinced himself he could go through with it and live with his decision, but now that he had, he found he was unable to look any of them in the eye. Even Bernard had peeled away into the main group and was glaring at him in disbelief, leaving Garrett standing alone.

"Look, I'm sorry…" he said, then let the words fade to nothing. He wanted to explain, to make them see his reasons, but there were no more words that seemed suitable. No matter how he tried to angle it, there was no justification, no explanation he could give other than selfish ones. He looked at them, and each time he made eye contact felt like a hammer blow.

"Donald, I…"

Donald spat in Garrett's face, his eyes glaring and fierce. Nicu simply watched it unfold, amused as Garrett wiped the mucus from his eyes.

"You're worse than them, Ray. At least they're honest." He growled as Helen grasped his arm.

"I had no choice…"

"There's always a choice!" Donald raged. "I just hope your conscience can live with what you've done, you son of a bitch."

Garrett was desperate to explain, to do anything to ease the guilt which raced through him. He lowered his head and found even the corpse-littered floor was easier to look at than the accusing eyes of the group.

"And so," said Nicu cheerfully, "I believe that concludes our business. I am a man of my word, Mr. Garrett. And as I said, to deny the world of somebody with your unique brand of selfishness would be a crime. So go. Go to your freedom. A prize you have truly earned."

Nicu gave the briefest of nods to the mountain-sized butcher, who immediately stepped out of the tunnel and moved aside.

"Go down the tunnel," Nicu said as Garrett paused at the threshold.

"You will eventually surface through a sewer outlet pipe by the river. From there, go back to your life. Live well and enjoy the fruits of tonight's labour. But take warning." Nicu leaned close, his face by Garrett's, his breath hot in Ray's ear. "You may feel the urge to tell people of what has happened here tonight, and that is your decision to make. But know this."

Nicu stepped back and held up a warning finger.

"Even though you are free, we will *always* be watching you. Just remember, our kind has infiltrated every level of your society. You will never know who it is safe to talk to, who you can trust, or who you can rely on. I wouldn't like to think I have made a mistake in allowing you to live."

"I already told you. All I want is to be with my family. Besides, I have too much blood on my hands as it is to ever be able to tell anyone about this. I just want to go home."

Nicu nodded. "Then go. Go into the world, Mr. Garrett, and enjoy the gift I have given you."

"Gift?"

"The gift of appreciation."

He smiled and stroked Leena's trembling cheek with a long, bony finger.

"I don't understand what you mean."

"You have tasted death. You have seen a small glimpse of another world that lives in secret alongside your own. From this day forth, you will appreciate every waking moment of what remains of your life, because you know intimately how fine the balance is between what you will have, and what could have been."

There was so much that Garrett wanted to say, so much he wanted to explain to the people that had thought of him as a friend, people he had then betrayed in the worst possible way. However, there were no words. Not that he knew, or would be able to articulate if he did. He stepped into to the tunnel and then turned back to Nicu.

"How many of you are there in the world. Your people, I mean?"

Nicu grinned, showing a glimpse of his pointed second set of teeth as his family members moved towards Garrett's group.

"There are more than you might think, Mr. Garrett. You might not recognise the name above the door, but every city has a Grueber's, in purpose if not in name. You should bear that in mind."

Garrett nodded and then turned back towards the tunnel, careful not to make eye contact with his group. He took a deep breath, and even though it went against every fibre of his being, entered its dark maw. He walked, and hoped he would be far enough away not to hear it when it happened, but he was wrong, and as those wet tearing sounds and agonised screams bounced off the walls around him, he found himself walking faster and then breaking into a loping run. He was not a religious man, but he prayed anyway. Prayed Nicu stuck to his word. Prayed that when the screams silenced, Nicu wasn't still hungry. Prayed he could trust the word of a foul, unearthly creature not to dangle the carrot of freedom in front of him, and then hunt him down and tear him limb from limb anyway, because hope made the meat sweeter. Right now it was all Garrett had. He could still hear the screams reverberating off the tunnel walls, and he wondered absently why they were still so loud despite his progress into the black depths. It was only then he realised the screams were coming from him.

Garrett lowered his head and started to sprint.

AUTHOR NOTES

This edition of *Meat* has been on my mind for some time. Initially, it was a story idea intended to go into *Dark Corners*, but I quickly realised after starting to write that it was going to be much too big for a collection, and it eventually grew into the novella that was released in December 2012. I like the story, I love the character interaction, but since it was released, something had been nagging at me. Even though the short story had become a slightly longer story, I still felt there was more to tell. Those early restrictions I had set on myself in order to keep the story short had stayed with me as I composed it, and there were more areas I wanted to explore. I also wanted to change a few things and make a few edits to the original manuscript. I toyed with perhaps exploring these areas with a sequel, but didn't really want to do that, as I felt although there was more to tell, I didn't think there was enough to justify another visit to Grueber's. As is my way, I mulled on it and stewed on it, and even tried to ignore it, but I couldn't stop the little voice nagging away in the back of my mind reminding me there was more story to tell here, and it really needed my attention.

It was later when I was speaking to a fellow author and friend of mine, who suggested perhaps I should release an extended edition, a director's cut if you will, of the story with all of the things I wanted to add to the story. It was a eureka moment, and with much excitement, I dusted off the original manuscript and began to look at how and where to fit in all of the things I wanted to do.

Now I openly acknowledge that some might prefer the original novella, and that's absolutely fine with me. I'm not releasing this as the definitive edition of the story, this is simply an alternate edit of the same story that some might enjoy.

For me, personally, I much prefer this version. This is the story as I wanted to tell it. I also like to think that with a lot more writing behind me since I first wrote the story, I have improved enough to refine the original text of the novella.

Some people have said they find the ending too bleak, and Garrett's betrayal a surprise. To that, I say re-read the story again after knowing how it turned out and the clues are plenty that Ray Garrett is a man who would do anything to survive. Some of the other characters within the story also saw it in him. Mark saw through Garrett for who he was around halfway into the story, he just, unfortunately, lost the battle to retain his sanity before he could help. Then, of course, there is Bernard. The man who was painted as the villain, who, granted was an irritating son of a bitch, might have been the hero of the piece after all. He might have gone off track and committed murder in the end, but I like to think he and Garrett weren't too dissimilar. Both were desperate to escape, both were natural leaders, the difference, in the end, was that Garrett made a deal with the devil whereas Bernard didn't. Take from that what you will.

If there is one question I have been asked countless times since I finished this story, it has to be the one around Garrett and if he made his escape. I think I know the answer, however, I'll keep that to myself. I think I like leaving his fate up to the imagination of you, the reader. Who knows, maybe one day, we will return to Grueber's and answer that question one way or the other. Until then, I'll leave it for you to decide.

    Michael
    15th of June, 2014

www.ingramcontent.com/pod-product-compliance
Lightning Source LLC
LaVergne TN
LVHW011942070526
838202LV00054B/4758